KT-457-305

FROM PARADISE...
TO PREGNANT!

FROM PARADISE...
TO PREGNANT!

BY

KANDY SHEPHERD

All rights reserved including the right of reproduction in whole or in part in any form. This edition is published by arrangement with Harlequin Books S.A.

This is a work of fiction. Names, characters, places, locations and incidents are purely fictional and bear no relationship to any real life individuals, living or dead, or to any actual places, business establishments, locations, events or incidents. Any resemblance is entirely coincidental.

This book is sold subject to the condition that it shall not, by way of trade or otherwise, be lent, resold, hired out or otherwise circulated without the prior consent of the publisher in any form of binding or cover other than that in which it is published and without a similar condition including this condition being imposed on the subsequent purchaser.

® and TM are trademarks owned and used by the trademark owner and/or its licensee. Trademarks marked with ® are registered with the United Kingdom Patent Office and/or the Office for Harmonisation in the Internal Market and in other countries.

First published in Great Britain 2015
by Mills & Boon, an imprint of Harlequin (UK) Limited,
Large Print edition 2015
Eton House, 18-24 Paradise Road,
Richmond, Surrey, TW9 1SP

© 2015 Kandy Shepherd

ISBN: 978-0-263-25691-8

C460426494

Harlequin (UK) Limited's policy is to use papers that are natural, renewable and recyclable products and made from wood grown in sustainable forests. The logging and manufacturing processes conform to the legal environmental regulations of the country of origin.

Printed and bound in Great Britain
by CPI Antony Rowe, Chippenham, Wiltshire

To my husband James for the trip to Bali
and the answers to my endless questions
about 'The Beautiful Game'.

CHAPTER ONE

ZOE SUMMERS KNEW she wasn't beautiful. The evidence of her mirror proved that. *Plain* was the label she'd been tagged with from an early age. She wasn't *ugly*—in fact ugly could be interesting. It was just that her particular combination of unruly black hair, angular face, regulation brown eyes and a nose with a slight bump in the middle added up to pass-under-the-radar plain.

After a particularly harrowing time in her life, spent at the basement level of the high school pecking order, she'd decided to do something about her unremarkable looks. Not a makeover, as such—rather, she'd aimed to make the best of herself and establish her own style. Now, at the age of twenty-seven, Zoe Summers was known as striking, stylish and smart. She couldn't ask for more than that.

As a consequence of her devotion to good grooming she'd spent some time every day of her vacation on the beautiful tropical island of Bali in the spa of her luxury villa hotel.

Back home, fitting in beauty treatments around running her own accountancy and taxation business could be problematic for a self-confessed workaholic. Here, a programme that included facials, exfoliation, waxing, manicure and pedicure fitted right in with her mission to relax and replenish. And all for less than half the price of what it would cost in Sydney.

Late on the fourth and final afternoon of her vacation, she lay face-down on a massage table in the spa and let the masseuse work her skilled magic on the tight knots of tension in her shoulders. *Bliss.*

As she breathed in the soothing scents of sandalwood, frangipani and lemongrass her thoughts started to drift. She diverted them from anything to do with her business and the decisions she still had to make. Or from the very real concern that her cat had gone on hunger strike at the cat boarding place.

Instead she pondered how soon after her massage she could take a languorous swim in the cool turquoise waters of the hotel's lagoon pool. What to choose for dinner at one of the many restaurants in Seminyak. Should she buy that lovely batik print sundress in the nearby boutique? Or the bikini? Or both? The price tags bore an astonishing number of Indonesian rupiah, but in Australian dollars they were as cheap as chips.

She sighed a deep sigh of contentment and relaxed into that delicious state somewhere between consciousness and sleep.

When the massage table began to vibrate she thought at first, through her blissed-out brain, that it was part of the treatment. But then the windows rattled and the glass bottles of scented oils and lotions started to jiggle and clank. When the bottles crashed to the stone floor she jumped up from the table in alarm.

She knew before her masseuse's cry of, 'Earthquake!' what was happening.

It was an effort to stay on her feet when the floor moved beneath them like the deck of a boat on choppy waters. No use trying to hold on to the walls, because they seemed to flex inward. The masseuse darted under the protection of the wooden table. Zoe did the same.

She cowered with her knees scrunched up to her chest, heart pounding, swallowing against a great lump of fear, her hand gripping tightly to the girl's—she didn't know who'd grabbed whose hand first, but she was grateful for the comfort. The room shuddered around them for what seemed like for ever but was probably seconds, stopped, then shuddered again.

Finally everything went still. Cautiously, Zoe inched out from under the table. She nearly gagged on the combined scent of spilled aromatherapy oils. When the masseuse told her they had to head to an emergency meeting point she nodded, too choked with anxiety to actually reply.

She wanted to get out into the open ASAP. But she was naked—save for the flimsy paper panties she'd donned for the massage to protect her modesty—and her clothes and sandals were in an inaccessible closet. She snatched up the white towel that had covered her on the massage table and with clumsy, trembling fingers wrapped it around her, tucking it in as securely as she could. In bare feet, she picked her way around the shards of broken bottles on the floor, grabbed her handbag and followed the masseuse outside.

Still reeling with shock, Zoe hurried along the tropical plant-lined pathway that led from the spa to the main building and pool area of the hotel. To her intense relief there didn't appear to be a lot of damage. But her fear didn't dissipate. Once before disaster had struck from nowhere, changing her life for ever. Who knew what she could expect here?

During her stay she hadn't taken much notice of the other guests. Each villa was completely private, with high walls around it and its own lap pool. Now she was surprised at the number of people gathered for an emergency briefing in the open courtyard outside the reception area. She was the only one in the crowd to be clad in just a towel, but other people were in swimwear or wearing assorted hastily donned garments.

Could she get to her room? If she was going to die she didn't want it to be in a white standard-issue hotel towel.

The other guests were terrified too. She could see it in their grim faces, hear their concern in the murmur of conversation in several different languages.

The hotel manager took the floor to reassure them that the tremor was low on the Richter Scale of seismic activity. He told his guests that electricity had been knocked out but that the hotel emergency generators would soon kick in and it would be business as usual. There was no need to panic.

But what if there were aftershocks?

The manager's reassuring words did little to make Zoe's rapid heartbeat subside or her hands less clammy. It was time to get out of here, before any other disaster might strike. She'd seen the sights. She'd wound down. She'd been pampered from head to toe. Now she was anxious to get home.

She was just about to ask the manager if the airport was open when a man spoke from several rows of people behind her.

'Is there a tsunami warning?' he asked.

The word 'tsunami' was enough to strike renewed fear into Zoe's heart. But it wasn't the thought of an imminent tidal wave that kick-started her heartbeat into overdrive, it was the man's voice. Deep, confident, immediately familiar.

Mitch Bailey.

But it couldn't be. There must be lots of Australian-accented male voices in Seminyak. The west coast town was a popular vacation playground for Australians. Besides, it was ten years since she'd last heard that voice. She must be mistaken.

'No tsunami warning,' the manager replied to the man. 'There's no danger.'

'What about aftershocks?' The man asked the question she was too paralysed by fear to ask herself.

It sounded so like him.

'Not likely now,' said the manager. 'It was a small tremor.'

Zoe risked a quick glance behind her to identify the owner of the voice.

And froze.

It was Mitch Bailey, all right—right up at the back of the room. He was instantly recognisable: green eyes, dark blond hair, wearing a pair of blue checked board shorts and nothing else. His tanned, well-honed chest was bare. The blood drained from her face and her mouth went dry.

He was as handsome as he'd been at seventeen. *More handsome.* His face was more chiselled, more lived in, and his dark blond hair was cut spikily short—much shorter than when she had known him. He was tall, broad-shouldered, but lean, with well defined muscles. Then he'd been a suburban high school heart-throb. Now he was an international soccer star, who regularly topped magazine lists of 'The Sexiest Men Alive'.

She quickly turned back and ducked her head. *Dear heaven, don't let him recognise her.* He was part of a past she had chosen to put well behind her. She couldn't let him see her.

Zoe thought back to the first day she'd met him. Grieving over the death of her parents, in an accident that had also injured her, she'd been removed from her inner city home and her laid-back, no-uniform high school and dumped mid-term by her disapproving grandmother— her father's mother—into an outer suburbs school where she'd known no one and no one had seemed to want to know her. The uniform had been scratchy, uncomfortable and hideous—which was just how she'd felt during her time at Northside High.

Her first sight of Mitch Bailey had been of him surrounded by girls, with his girlfriend Lara—blonde and beautiful, of course—hanging possessively onto his arm. Zoe had kept her head down and walked past. But a burst of chatter had made her lift her head and she'd caught his eye. He'd smiled. A friendly, open smile born of his place as kingpin of his social group. He'd been a jock, a sports star—the most popular of the popular boys.

He hadn't needed to smile at nerdy *her*. But he had, and it had warmed the chill of her frozen heart even though she'd been unable to manage more than a polite stretching of her lips in return.

Later they'd become sort of friends, when he'd had a problem she'd been able to help him with. But the last time she'd seen him he'd been so unforgivably hurtful she'd shrivelled back into her shell and stayed there until she'd got out of that school. Now she had no desire to make contact again with anyone from that place—least of all with him.

She tensed, her eyes darting around for an escape route, then realised her panic was for nothing. No way would he recognise her. She looked completely different from the unhappy seventeen-year-old he'd befriended all those years ago. But she kept her eyes to the ground anyway.

She wanted to ask the manager about the airport as she was due to fly back to Sydney the next morning. But she didn't want to draw attention to herself. If she'd recognised his voice, Mitch might recognise hers. It was unlikely, but possible. She kept her mouth shut just in case.

The manager had said it was okay for the guests to return to their villas. That was where she was headed—pronto.

As other people started to ask more questions Zoe inched to the edge of the group. Not meeting anyone's gaze, and as unobtrusively as she could, she edged away towards the pathway that led to her private villa. Once there she could order room service for the rest of her stay, to make sure she didn't bump into Mitch Bailey.

Please, please don't let him be anywhere around when she checked out.

She quickened her pace as she got near the pathway.

'Zoe?'

His voice came from behind her and she started. She denied the reflex that would have had her turning around. Instead she kept her head down and kept walking, hoping against hope that he wouldn't call her name again. *Let him think he'd been mistaken.*

Mitch had noticed the dark-haired girl wrapped in a white towel as soon as she'd come into the courtyard. What red-blooded male wouldn't? The skimpy towel barely covered a sensational body.

It was knotted between high, round breasts and fell just to the top of slender, tanned thighs. Might it fall off at any moment? And, if so, was she wearing anything underneath? He'd been lying by his pool when the earthquake had hit. What had *she* been doing to be clad only in a towel?

But he'd thought no more about it as the girl had found a place near the front of the group of guests who had gathered to hear the charming Balinese hotel manager explain the ramifications of the earth tremor.

Mitch had been to Bali before, and knew small tremors like this weren't uncommon. He'd appreciated the manager's well-meant reassurances. But still, he'd asked the question about the tsunami because it didn't pay to ignore possible danger. Mitch was the kind of guy who liked to anticipate and prepare for the next move— 'reading the play', they called it in soccer. There was a prominent sign on the beach warning people what to do if there was a tsunami warning. Therefore he'd needed to ask about it.

At his second enquiry the girl in the towel had turned briefly, to see who was asking the scary questions. Recognition had flashed just briefly before she had hastily turned back round.

He was used to that these days. Strangers recognised him as being an international soccer player. Or from the endorsements for designer menswear and upscale watches he'd posed for—the advertisements were on billboards even here in Bali. This woman might be a young mum who wanted him to sign her child's soccer ball. Or a fan with much more than signing on her mind.

He narrowed his eyes. The thing was, she had also seemed familiar to him. Her eyes had only caught his for a split second but there had been something about the expression in them—anxious, in a pale, drawn face—that had tugged at his memory. He'd met so many people over the last years, but he couldn't place her. He'd dredged his memory with no luck.

But then she'd hotfooted it away from the group of guests. He'd admired her shapely behind, swaying in that tightly drawn towel as she'd headed for the pathway that led to the private villas. Once she was gone he'd probably never see her again, and would be left wondering who she could possibly have been.

Then he'd noticed the slight, almost imperceptible limp as she'd favoured her right leg. It was enough to trigger memories of a girl he'd known for a short time in high school.

'Zoe!' he'd called.

She'd paused for a moment, her shoulders set rigidly. Then continued to walk away.

Now he pushed his way to the edge of the row of people and took a few strides towards her to catch up.

'Zoe Summers?' he asked, raising his voice.

This time she stopped and turned to face him. For a long moment their gazes met. Mitch was shocked to realise she had recognised him and yet had chosen to walk away. He was swept by conflicting feelings—the most predominant being shame. It was what he deserved after the way he'd treated her all those years ago.

'Mitch Bailey,' she said, head tilted, no trace of a welcoming smile. 'After all this time.'

'I knew it was you,' he said.

Her expression told him a kiss on the cheek, a hug, even a handshake would not be welcome. He kept his hands to his sides.

She looked much the same. More grown-up, of course. But the same sharp, intelligent face.

The same black hair—only shorter now, and all tousled around her face. The piercings she'd sported so defiantly at school had gone, leaving tiny telltale holes along the top of her right eyebrow and in her nose, and there was just one pair of discreet gold studs in her ears instead of multiple hoops.

There was something indefinably different about her. Perhaps it was her air of assuredness. He didn't remember that. Back then she'd emanated a miasma of misery that had made other adolescents uncomfortable around her. The 'keep away' glower hadn't helped either. He'd considered himself privileged to have discovered the amazing person behind it all. Until he'd blown their friendship.

'I didn't think you'd recognise me,' she said.

He'd forgotten what an appealing voice she had: mellow, slightly husky.

'You mean you hoped I wouldn't.' He'd intended his words to sound light-hearted, but they came out flat.

She shrugged. 'I didn't say that. It's been years.'

He swallowed uncomfortably. 'Strange way to meet again. In an earthquake.'

'A "tremor" the management called it,' she said with a wry twist to her lips. 'Playing it down so as not to freak out the tourists.'

'Whatever name you give it, it scared the day-lights out of me.'

She reacted with a raising of her perfectly shaped black eyebrows. 'Me too,' she said, with the shadow of a smile. 'I thought my end had come. Still think it's a possibility.'

'Where were you when the quake struck?'

'Having a body massage down at the spa.'

Where she must have been naked. So that was why she had only a towel wrapped around her.

Mitch willed his eyes to stay above her neck. Before today he'd only ever seen Zoe in a shape-less school uniform. He hadn't taken much notice of her body back then—it was her brain that had interested him. Besides, he'd had a girlfriend. Now he realised what great shape Zoe was in—in her own quiet way she was hot.

'Where were *you* when it hit?' she asked.

'Just about to dive into my lap pool. Then I

noticed the surface of the water shimmering, which was kind of weird.'

'That must have been scary.' She shuddered as she spoke.

'Yeah. It was.'

'So much for relaxing in a tropical paradise,' she said, with a bravado that didn't hide the shadow of unease in her eyes.

She clutched her towel tighter to her. Mitch refused to let himself imagine what might happen if it slid off.

An awkward silence fell between them. Zoe was the first to break it. 'I'm going to head back to my villa,' she said.

'How about I come with you? Who knows what we'll find when we get back to our rooms.'

Her response was more of a cynical twist than a smile, but it was nonetheless attractive. 'Thank you, but I don't need a big strong man to protect me. I'm quite capable of looking after myself.'

'I'm sure you are,' he said. 'But I… Well, I don't really want to be on my own if we get any aftershocks.'

He wasn't afraid to admit to vulnerability. Just never on a football pitch.

'Oh,' she said.

For the first time she seemed flustered.

'You're not...you're not with someone?'

'You mean a girlfriend? No. What about you? Are you on your own?'

'Yes,' she said, with no further explanation.

He glanced down at her hand. No wedding ring. Though that didn't necessarily mean no man in her life. 'I'd like to catch up, Zoe. Find out what you've been doing in the last ten years.'

She paused. 'I don't need to ask what you've done since we last met,' she said. 'You're quite the sporting hero. The media loves you.'

He shrugged. 'Yeah... That... Don't believe everything they dish up about me. But seriously, Zoe, I'd really like to spend some time with you.'

Zoe looked up at him and her heart gave a flip of awareness. Mitch Bailey. Still the same: so handsome, so unselfconscious, standing before her in just a pair of swim shorts that did nothing to hide the athletic perfection of his body.

So full of the innate confidence that came with the knowledge that he had always been liked, admired, wanted. So sure she'd want to spend time with him.

And she'd be lying to herself if she said she didn't.

He was the best-looking man she'd ever met. Had been then—still was now. She couldn't deny that. But all those years ago she'd seen a more vulnerable side of Mitch that had endeared him to her before he'd pushed her out of his life. Had it survived his stardom? It was difficult to resist the chance to find out.

'I'd like to catch up too,' she said lightly. 'After all, it isn't every day an earthquake brings long-lost school buddies together.'

He didn't seem to remember the circumstances of their last meeting. It had been a long time ago. Devastating to her at the time. Insignificant, it seemed, to him.

Had she had a crush on him back then? Of course she had. A deeply hidden, secret, impossible crush. He'd been so out of her league she would have been relentlessly mocked if anyone had found out.

'Great,' he said with a smile.

If she didn't know better, she'd think it was tinged with relief.

'The manager said it was business as usual. We can order drinks. I don't know about you, but I could do with a beer.'

'Me too,' she said.

And the first thing she'd do before she spent any more time alone with Mitch Bailey would be to put on some clothes.

CHAPTER TWO

ZOE'S VILLA HAD suffered minimal damage from the tremor—just a few glasses she'd left out had smashed to the tiled floor. Still, it was a shock—a reminder of how much worse it could have been. Might yet be.

She wanted to clear up the broken glass. But she felt awkward dressed only in the towel and she still felt very shaky. For every piece she picked up, she dropped another.

Mitch insisted he do it for her. Thanking him, she escaped into her bedroom and pulled closed the door that divided the room from the living area. The villa was like a roomy one-bedroom apartment, with all the external doors folding back to access the enclosed courtyard and private lap pool.

Her heart was thumping like crazy. Residual fear from the earthquake? More likely the effect of being in close proximity to Mitch Bailey.

She hadn't *stalked* him over the years. Not that. But when a boy she'd gone to school with had shot to fame she wouldn't have been human if she hadn't read the magazine stories, watched the television interviews, cheered for him when he'd been the youngest ever player in the Australian Socceroos team for the World Cup.

All the while she'd been getting on with her life—first studying, then working, dating, and only ever thinking about him when the media brought him to her attention.

Now he'd been thrust into her life again. And she was clad in a towel, with no make-up on and her hair all mussed up with massage oil.

Hastily she pulled on a sleekly cut black bikini, then slid into a simple sleeveless dress in an abstract black-and-white print. It fell to just above her knees. The humid tropical heat made anything else uncomfortable. She pulled a brush through her hair and slicked on a natural toned lipstick.

Did she want to look her best for Mitch? Her 'best' involved twenty minutes in front of a mirror with a make-up kit and heated hair tongs.

She shouldn't be worried about how she looked now; he'd seen her at her worst ten years ago. She shuddered at the memory of what she'd looked like back then. The mono-brow. The bushy hair. The prone-to-eruption skin.

But still, she wished today she could look her usual polished, poised self. Her best self. There was no denying she'd feel more confident with straightened hair and more make-up. But she didn't want to waste time fussing over her appearance when she could be catching up with Mitch. Who knew when she'd see him again— if ever?

He'd switched on the television in the living area and was watching the screen when she came back out of her bedroom.

'The manager was right—there's minimal disruption,' he said. 'Seems like Bali gets small tremors like this quite often. But the risk of aftershocks is real.'

Aftershocks. She knuckled her hand against her mouth to suppress a gasp; she didn't want to appear too fearful. Not when Mitch seemed so laid back about the risk.

He switched off the TV and turned to face her. Had he grown taller since she'd last stood so near to him? They were both in their bare feet. He seemed to stand about six-foot-one to her five-foot-five.

Six-foot-one of total hotness.

Mitch was an elite sportsman in his prime, and he had celebrity status with as many fans as any actor or musician.

Her proximity to his bare chest was doing nothing to slow down her revved-up heartbeat. If she'd had a T-shirt big enough to stretch over all those muscles, she would have offered to lend it to him. But wouldn't it be a crime to cover that expanse of buff body?

She wanted to take a step back, but didn't want to signal how disconcerted she felt by said buff body being so close to her. Instead she stood her ground and forced her voice to sound controlled and conversational.

'So this region sometimes gets harmless tremors? That didn't stop it from being frightening, though, did it?' she said. 'I huddled under the massage table, making all sorts of bargains with myself about what I'd do if I got out safely.'

'What kind of bargains?' he asked.

'Spend more time with friends and less at work. Give more to charity.' She shrugged. 'Stuff that wouldn't interest you.'

His eyes were as green as she remembered them, and now they looked intently into hers. 'How do you know they wouldn't interest me?' he said, in a voice that seemed to have got an octave deeper.

A shiver of awareness tingled through her. *Sexiest man alive, all right.*

'Our lives are so different. It's like we inhabit different spaces on the planet,' she said.

'What do you think is my space on the planet?'

'Spain? I believe you play for one of the top Spanish teams. I've never been to Spain.'

'I live in Madrid.'

'There you go. I still live in Sydney. Fact is, the air you breathe is way more rarefied than mine.'

'I don't know if that's true or not. We're both staying in the same hotel.'

'My booking was a last-minute bargain on the internet. Yours?'

He smiled. The same appealing, slightly uneven smile he'd had at the age of seventeen. 'Maybe not.'

'That's just my point. You're famous. Not just for being a brilliant football player but for being handsome, wealthy, and photographed with a different gorgeous woman on your arm every time you're seen in public.'

And they were all tall, blonde and beautiful clones of Lara, back in high school.

'That's where you have an unfair advantage over me,' he said. 'You've read about me in the media—seen me on TV, perhaps. That's not to say what you've seen is the truth. But I know nothing about what's happened to you since we were at Northside High.'

'Because we occupy different space on the planet,' she repeated, determined to make her point. 'I went to another school after Northside, but I was still in Sydney. Away from school I hung out in the same clubs and went to the same concerts as other kids our age. But our paths never crossed again.'

'Until now,' he said.

'Yes. It took an earthquake to shake us back into the same space.'

He laughed, and she had to smile in response.

'You've still got a quirky way of putting things. Seriously, Zoe, I want to know all about you,' he said.

His words were flattering, seductive. Not seductive in a sexual way, but in a way that tempted her to open up and confide in him because he sounded as though her answer was important to him. That *she* was important to him. Even aged seventeen he'd had that gift of being totally focussed on the person he was addressing.

She realised it was highly unlikely she'd see Mitch again after today. He would go home to Madrid; she would fly back to Sydney. There was also a chance that a bigger earthquake might hit and the whole resort area would be wiped out. It was unnerving in one way—liberating in another.

'How about we get that beer and then we can talk?' she said.

'About you?'

'And you too,' she said, finding it impossible not to feel flattered. 'I'd like to hear about your life behind those media reports.'

'If that's what you want.'

'I'm warning you: my life story will be quite mundane compared to yours.'

'Let me be the judge of that,' he said.

'There are beers in the mini-bar,' she said. 'I've been on an alcohol-free detox since I've been in Bali and sticking with mineral water. Not that I drink a lot,' she hastened to add.

'I think getting out of an earthquake unscathed is reason enough to break your fast,' he said, heading towards the fridge.

He brought out two bottles of the local Indonesian beer, took off the caps and handed one to her.

'Let's take them out near the pool,' she said, picking up one of the remaining glasses to take with her. The ceiling fans were circulating air around the rooms, but the air-conditioning didn't appear to be back on yet. Besides, it felt too intimate to be alone in here with Mitch, and the king-sized bed was too clearly in view.

It was only a few steps out to the rectangular lap pool, which was edged on three sides with plantings of broad-leaved tropical greenery. Two smart, comfortable wooden sun loungers with blue-striped mattresses sat side by side in the shade of a frangipani tree. A myriad of pink flowers had been shaken off the tree by the quake onto the loungers and into the water. The petals floated on the turquoise surface of the pool in picture-perfect contrast.

In different circumstances Zoe would have taken a photo of how pretty they looked. Instead she placed the beer bottle and the glass on the small wooden table between the two loungers. She flicked off the flowers that had settled on one lounger before she sat down, her back supported, her legs stretched out in front of her. Thank heaven for all that waxing, moisturising and toenail-painting that had gone on in the spa yesterday.

She felt very conscious of Mitch settling into

the lounger on her right. His legs were lean, with tightly defined muscles, his classic six-pack belly hard and flat. Even she knew soccer players trained for strength, speed and agility rather than for bulky muscle. Come to think of it, she might know that from hearing him being interviewed on the subject at some stage…

These villas were often booked by honeymooners, she knew. The loungers were set as close as they could be, with only that narrow little table separating them. Loved-up couples could easily touch in complete privacy.

She had never touched Mitch, she realised. Not a hug. Not even a handshake. Certainly not a kiss. Not even a chaste, platonic kiss on the cheek. It just hadn't been appropriate back then. Now she had to resist the urge to reach out and put her hand on his arm. Not in a sexual way, or even a friendly way. Just to reassure herself that he was real, he was here, that they were both alive.

She and Mitch Bailey.

He swigged his beer straight from the bottle. The way he tilted back his head, the arch of his neck, made the simple act of drinking a beer look as if he was doing it for one of those advertisements he starred in.

He was graceful. That was what it was. Graceful in a strong, sleek, utterly masculine way. She didn't remember that from the last time she'd seen him. Off the football field he'd been more gauche than graceful. At seventeen he hadn't quite grown into his long limbs and big feet. Since then he'd trained with the best sports trainers in the world.

Yes, he inhabited not just a different space but a different planet from her. But for this time— maybe an hour, maybe a few hours—their planets had found themselves in the same orbit.

Mitch put down his beer. 'So, where did you go when you left our school?' he asked. 'You just seemed to disappear.'

Zoe felt a stab of pain that he didn't seem to remember their last meeting. But if he wasn't going to mention it she certainly wasn't. Even now dragging it out of the recesses where her hurts were hidden was painful.

She poured beer into her glass. Took a tentative sip. Cold. Refreshing. Maybe it would give her the Dutch courage she so sorely needed to mine her uncomfortable memories of the past. She considered herself to be a private person. She didn't spill her soul easily.

'I won a scholarship to a private girls' boarding school in the eastern suburbs. I started there for the next term.'

'You always were a brainiac,' he said, with what seemed to be genuine admiration.

Zoe didn't deny it. She'd excelled academically and had been proud of her top grades—not only in maths and science but also in languages and music. But if there'd been such a thing as a social report card for her short time at Northside she would have scored a big, fat fail. She'd had good friends at her old inner city school, an hour's train ride away, but her grandmother had thwarted her efforts to see them. The only person who had come anywhere near to being a friend at Northside had been Mitch.

'I had to get away from my grandmother. Getting the scholarship was the only way I could do it.'

'How did she react?'

'Furious I'd gone behind her back. But glad to get rid of me.'

Mitch frowned. 'You talk as though she hated you?'

'She did.' It was a truth she didn't like to drag out into the sunlight too often.

'Surely not? She was your *grandma*.'

Mitch came from a big, loving family. No wonder he found it difficult to comprehend the aridity of her relationship with her grandmother.

'She blamed me for the death of my father.'

Mitch was obviously too shocked to speak for a long moment. 'But you weren't driving the car. Or the truck that smashed into it.'

He remembered.

She was stunned that Mitch recalled her telling him about the accident that had killed her parents and injured her leg so badly she still walked with a slight limp when she was very tired or stressed. They'd been heading north to a music festival in Queensland; just her and the mother and father she'd adored. A truck-driver had fallen asleep at the wheel and veered onto their side of a notoriously bad stretch of the Pacific Highway.

'No. I was in the back seat. I...I'm surprised you remember.'

He slowly shook his head. 'How could I forget? It seemed the most terrible thing to have happened to a kid. I loved my family. I couldn't have managed without them.'

Zoe shifted in her seat. She hated people pitying her. 'You felt sorry for me?'

'Yes. And sad for you too.'

There was genuine compassion on his handsome famous face, and she acknowledged the kindness of his words with a slight silent nod. As a teenager she'd sensed a core of decency behind his popular boy image. It was why she'd been so shocked at the way he'd treated her at the end.

As she'd watched his meteoric rise she'd wondered if fame and the kind of adulation he got these days had changed him. Who was the real Mitch?

Here, now, in the aftermath of an earthquake, maybe she had been given the chance to find out.

CHAPTER THREE

WERE THERE ELEPHANTS in Bali? There were lots of monkeys; Mitch knew that from his visit to the Ubud area in the highlands.

He'd heard there were elephants indigenous to the neighbouring Indonesian island of Sumatra that had been trained to play soccer. But he would rather see elephants in their natural habitat, dignified and not trained to do party tricks.

Whether or not there were elephants on Bali, there was an elephant in the room with him and Zoe. Or rather, an elephant in the pool. A large metaphorical elephant, wallowing in the turquoise depths, spraying water through its trunk in an effort to get their attention.

Metaphorical.

Zoe had taught him how to use that term.

The elephant was that last day they'd seen each other, ten years ago. He'd behaved badly. Lashed out at her. Humiliated her. Hadn't defended her against Lara's cattiness. He'd felt rotten about it once he'd cooled down. But he had never got the chance to apologise. He owed her that. He also owed her thanks for the events that had followed.

Zoe hadn't said anything, but he'd bet she remembered the incident. He could still see her face as it had crumpled with shock and hurt. He mightn't have been great with words when it came to essays, but his words to her had wounded; the way he'd allowed her to be mocked by Lara had been like an assault.

Now Zoe sat back on the lounger next to him, her slim, toned legs stretched out in front of her. He didn't remember her being a sporty girl at school. But she must exercise regularly to keep in such great shape. It seemed she hadn't just changed in appearance. Zoe was self-possessed, composed—in spite of the fact they'd just experienced an earthquake. Though he suspected a fear of further tremors lay just below her self-contained surface.

'I want to clear the air,' he said.

'What...what do you mean?' she said.

But the expression in her dark brown eyes told

him she knew exactly what he meant. Knew and hadn't forgotten a moment of it.

'About what a stupid young idiot I was that last day. Honest. I didn't know that would be the last time I'd see you.'

Mitch was the youngest of four sons in a family of high achievers. His brothers had excelled academically; he'd excelled at sport. That had been his slot in the family. His parents hadn't worried about his mediocre grades at school. The other boys were to be a lawyer, an accountant and a doctor respectively. Mitch had been the sportsman. They could boast about him—they hadn't expected more from him.

But Mitch had expected more of himself. He'd been extremely competitive. Driven to excel. If his anointed role was to be the sportsman, he'd be the *best* sportsman.

The trouble was, the school had expected him to do more than concentrate on soccer in winter and basketball in summer. With minimal effort he'd done okay in maths, science and geography—not top grades, but not the lowest either. It had been English he couldn't get his head around.

And English had been a compulsory subject for the final Higher School Certificate.

His teenage brain hadn't seen the point of studying long-dead authors and playwrights. Of not just reading contemporary novels but having to analyse the heck out of them. And then there was poetry. He hadn't been able to get it. He hadn't wanted to get it. It had been bad enough having to study it. He sure as hell hadn't been going to write the poem required as part of his term assessment. He *couldn't* write a poem.

Zoe Summers hadn't been in his English class. No way. The new girl nerd was in the top classes for everything. But during a study period in the library she'd been sitting near him when he'd flung his poetry book down on the floor, accompanied by a string of curses that had drawn down the wrath of the supervising librarian.

The other kids had egged him on and laughed. He'd laughed too. But it hadn't been a joke. If he didn't keep up a decent grade average for English he wasn't going to be allowed to go to a week-long soccer training camp that cut into the school term by a couple of days. He'd been determined to get to that camp.

The teenage Zoe had caught his eye when he had leaned down to pick up his book from the floor. She'd smiled a shy smile and murmured, 'Can I help? I'm such a nerd I actually *like* poetry.'

Help? No one had actually offered to help him before. And he'd had too much testosterone-charged teenage pride to ask for it.

'I'll be right here in the library after school,' she'd said. 'Meet me here if you want me to help.'

He'd hesitated. He couldn't meet her in public. Not the jock and the nerd. A meeting between them would mean unwanted attention. Mockery. Insults. Possible spiteful retaliation from Lara. He could handle all that, but he had doubted Zoe could.

His hesitation must have told her that.

'Or you could meet me at my house after school,' she'd said, in such a low tone only he could have heard it.

She'd scribbled something on a piece of paper and passed it unobtrusively to him. He'd taken it. Nodded. Then turned back to his mates. Continued to crack jokes and be generally disruptive until he'd been kicked out of the library.

But he had still needed to pass that poetry assignment. He had decided to take Zoe up on her offer of help. No matter the consequences.

Her house had been just two streets away from his, in the leafy, upmarket northern suburb of Wahroonga. Their houses had looked similar from the outside, set in large, well-tended gardens. Inside, they couldn't have been more different.

His house had been home to four boys: he still at school, the others at universities in Sydney. There'd been a blackboard in the well-used family room, where all family members had chalked up their whereabouts. The house had rung with lots of shouting and boisterous ribbing by the brothers and their various friends.

Zoe's house had been immaculate to the point of sterility. Straight away he'd been able to tell she was nervous when she'd greeted him at the front door. He'd soon seen why. An older woman she'd introduced as her grandmother had hovered behind her, mouth pinched, eyes cold. He'd never felt more unwelcome.

The grandma had told Zoe to entertain her visitor in the dining room, with the door open at all times. Mitch had felt unnerved—ready to bolt back the way he'd come. But then Zoe had rolled her eyes behind her grandmother's back and pulled a comical face.

They'd established a connection. And in the days that had followed he'd got to like and respect Zoe as she had helped him tackle his dreaded poetry assignment.

'I want to explain what happened back then,' he said now.

Zoe shrugged. 'Does it matter after all this time?' she said, her voice tight, not meeting his eyes.

It did to him. She had helped him. He had let her down.

'Do you remember how hard you worked to help me get my head around poetry?' he asked.

'You were the one doing all the work. I just guided you in the right direction.'

He slammed down his hand on the edge of the

lounger in remembered anger. 'That's exactly right. You made me use my own words—not yours. It was unfair.'

'What...what exactly happened in the classroom that day?'

'The teacher had had the assignment for a week. So I was on edge, waiting to see if I'd passed or not. By then it had become something more than just wanting to go to the soccer camp. She handed out the marked essays, desk by desk. She saved mine for last.'

'You should have easily passed. By that time we'd spent so much time on it—you really understood it.'

'I thought I'd understood it, too. She got to my desk. Held up the paper for everyone to see the great big "Fail" scrawled across it. Told the class I was a cheat. Read out my grade and added her comments for maximum humiliation.'

The look on that teacher's face was still seared into his memory.

Before he'd studied with Zoe he would have made a joke of it. Clowned around. Annoyed the teacher until she'd kicked him out of the classroom. But not that time. He'd deserved better.

'What happened?'

'I snatched the paper from the teacher's hand and stormed out.'

'To find me lurking outside in the corridor. Pretending I was waiting for a class to start in the next room. Ready to congratulate you on a brilliant pass. Instead I got in your way.'

He noticed how tightly she was gripping on to her glass. No wonder. He'd vented all his outraged adolescent anger and humiliation on her. It couldn't be a pleasant memory.

'Instead I behaved like a total jerk.'

'Yeah. You did. You...you thrust the paper in my face. I can still see that word written so big in red ink: "Plagiarism".'

'She thought I was too stupid to write such a good essay. And I took it out on you.'

He'd yelled at her that it was *her* fault. Told her to get out of his way. Never talk to him again. Had he actually shoved her? He didn't think so. His words had been as effective as any physical blow.

He'd seen her face crumple in disbelief, then pain, then schooled indifference as she'd walked away. She'd muttered that she was sorry—she'd only been trying to help. And he'd let her go.

Worse, a half-hour later he'd encountered Zoe again. This time he'd been hanging near the canteen, with his crowd of close friends and his girlfriend, Lara. Zoe had obviously been startled to see them. Startled and, he'd realised afterwards, alarmed. She'd immediately started to turn away, eyes cast down, shoulders hunched. But that hadn't been enough for Lara, who hadn't liked him studying with another girl one little bit.

'Buzz off, geek-girl,' Lara had sneered. 'Mitch doesn't need *your* kind of help. Not when he's got *me*.'

Then Lara had pulled his face to hers and given him a provocatively deep kiss. Her girlfriends had started to laugh and his mates had joined in, their laughter echoing through the corridors of the school.

He'd just kept on kissing Lara. When he'd finally pulled away Zoe had gone. It was only later that he'd realised how he'd betrayed her by his silence and inaction.

That had been ten years ago. Now she smiled that wry smile that was already becoming familiar. 'Teenage angst. Who'd go back there?'

'Teenage angst or not, I behaved badly. And after ten years I want to take this opportunity to say sorry. To see if there is any way I could make it up to you.'

Digging deep into feelings she'd rather were kept buried made Zoe feel uncomfortable. She found it impossible to meet Mitch's gaze. To gain herself a moment before she had to reply, she put her glass down onto the table and tugged her dress down over her thighs.

'We were just kids,' she said.

Though Lara's spite had been only too grown up. And the pain she'd felt when Mitch had ignored her hadn't been the pain of a child.

Truth was, the episode was a reminder of a particularly unhappy time in her life. She'd rather not be reminded of how she'd felt back then. That was why she had tried to avoid Mitch earlier on, when she'd first recognised him.

'I was old enough to know better,' he said.

Now she turned to face him. 'Seriously, if you hadn't always been popping up in the media I would have forgotten all about what happened. I'm cool with it.'

He persisted. 'I'm *not* cool with it. I want to make amends.'

She wished he would drop it. 'If it makes you feel any better, my experiences at Northside made me stronger—determined to change. No way was I going to be that miserable at my new school. I decided to do whatever it took to fit in.'

'Your piercings? Which, by the way, I used to think were kinda cute.'

'Gone. I wore the uniform straight up—exactly as prescribed. Put the "anything goes" lifestyle I'd enjoyed with my parents behind me. Played the private school game by their rules. I watched, learned and conformed.'

And it had worked. At the new academically elite school she hadn't climbed up the pecking order to roost with the 'popular' girls, but neither had she been one of the shunned.

'Was it the right move?'

Again she was conscious of his intent focus on her. As if he were really interested in her reply.

'Yes. I was happy there—did well, made some good friends.'

One in particular had taken the new girl under her wing and helped transform the caterpillar. Not into a gaudy butterfly, more an elegantly patterned moth who fitted perfectly into her surroundings.

'I'm glad to hear that. But I want you to know I feel bad about what happened. I want to right the wrong.'

Zoe shrugged, pretended indifference, but secretly she was chuffed. Mitch Bailey apologising? Mitch Bailey maybe even grovelling a tad? It was good. It was healing. It was—she couldn't deny it—*satisfying.*

'Consider it righted,' she said firmly. 'Apology accepted. You were young and disappointed and you took it out on the first person who crossed your path.'

'I tried to find you,' he said.

'You did?' she said, startled. That he'd remembered the incident at all in such detail was mind-boggling.

'After the soccer training camp I went away on vacation with my family. When I got back to school you weren't there. I went around to your house. Your grandmother told me you didn't live there any more. I thought she was going to slam the door in my face.'

'Sounds like my grandmother.'

'Remember how she always made you leave the door open and patrolled outside it? I felt like a criminal. Did she think I was going to steal the silver?'

'She was terrified you'd get me pregnant.'

Mitch nearly choked on his beer. He stared at her for a long, astounded moment. *'What?'*

Zoe waited for him to stop spluttering, resisting the temptation to pat him on that broad, muscular back. She probably shouldn't have shared that particular detail of her dysfunctional relationship with her grandmother.

She felt her cheeks flush pink as she explained. 'I told her we were just friends. I told her you had a girlfriend. That the only thing going on in that room was studying.'

Not to mention that Mitch Bailey wouldn't have looked at her as girlfriend material in a million years.

'Why the hell did she think—?'

'She wasn't going to let me—' Zoe made quote marks in the air with her fingers '—"get pregnant and ruin the future of some fine young man" the way my mother had ruined my father's. You counted as one of those fine young men. She knew of your family.'

How many times had her grandmother harangued her about that, over and over again, until she'd had to put her fingers in her ears to block out the hateful words?

Mitch frowned. 'What? I don't get it.'

Thank heaven back then her grandmother hadn't said anything to Mitch about the pregnancy thing. She would have been mortified beyond redemption.

'It sounds warped, doesn't it? I didn't get it either when I was seventeen. I thought she was insane. I'd adored my parents. They'd adored each other. But Mum was only nineteen when I was born. Because my father dropped out of his law degree my grandmother blamed my mother for seducing him, getting pregnant on purpose and ruining his life.'

'Whoa. You said your life story was *mundane*.' He paused, narrowed his eyes. 'And she transferred the blame to you, right?'

'Yep. If I hadn't come along her son would have got to be a lawyer.'

'And he wouldn't have died?'

'Correct.'

'That's irrational.'

'You could say that.'

'Yet she gave you a home?'

'Reluctantly. She couldn't even bear to look at me. I look like my dad, you see. A constant reminder of what she had lost. But she felt she had to do the right thing by her granddaughter.' In spite of herself a note of bitterness crept into her voice. 'After all, what would her golfing friends have thought?'

'Did you have any other family you could have gone to?'

'My mother's brother, whom I love to pieces. But as he has a propensity to dress in frocks sometimes the courts didn't approve of him as guardian to a minor.'

Mitch laughed. 'The lawyers must have had fun with that one.' He sobered. 'No wonder you were so miserable back then.'

The rejection by her grandmother had hurt. There had been no shared grief. No comfort. Just blame and bitterness. 'I did something about it, though,' she said.

'What could a kid of seventeen have done?'

'My new best friend at school—who incidentally is still my best friend—had a mother who was a top lawyer. She helped me get legal emancipation from my grandmother. There was compensation and insurance money from the accident that got signed over to me. I was able to support myself.'

He whistled. 'That was a tough thing to do. Brave too.'

She shrugged. 'My new life started then.'

'You had worse things going on than a teenage me ranting at you…'

She met his gaze. 'What happened with you hurt me. I won't deny it. I...I valued our friendship. It was a beacon in the darkness of those days.'

Mitch swore low and fluently.

She waited for him to finish. 'It's history now. I appreciate your apology. And I don't want to hear one more word about it.'

'Just a few more words,' he said, with that engaging grin.

'I can't imagine what more there is to be said,' she said, her lips twitching into a smile in response. 'But okay. Your final words. Fire away.'

'I was sent to the principal to be punished for my plagiarism. She was new that year and didn't know me. When I explained she listened. Turns out I had a mild form of dyslexia that had never been diagnosed. I got help. My grades picked up. Not just in English, but all my subjects. I could have gone to university on my Higher School Certificate results if I hadn't chosen to play soccer instead.'

'Mitch, that's wonderful news!'

Her instinct was to reach out and hug him.

With every fibre of her being she resisted it. She could not trust herself to touch him.

But while *she* thought touching was not on the agenda, Mitch obviously thought otherwise. He reached out and put his hand on her shoulder. 'I have a lot to thank you for, Zoe,' he said.

His hand was warm and firm on her bare skin and she had to force herself not to tremble with the pleasure of it.

She had to clear her throat before she could reply. 'Not me. The principal. Yourself. That's who you should thank.'

He let his hand drop from her shoulder and she felt immediately bereft of his touch. That attraction she'd felt for him at seventeen was still there, simmering below the surface.

'I'm determined to thank you, whether you acknowledge your role in the outcome or not,' he said. 'The least I can do is buy you dinner.' He looked at his watch. 'An early dinner?'

That threw her. She'd assumed once they'd sorted out the problems of the past he'd be on his way. 'Here? Now?'

'I don't think it would be a good idea to go

into Seminyak so soon after the quake. Too dangerous.'

'I…I was going to order room service,' she blurted out.

'I was going to suggest the hotel restaurant. But I might get recognised. And I don't want anyone else intruding on our reunion celebration. Room service is a great idea. Your villa or mine?'

'Uh… H-Here would be good,' she stammered. *Reunion celebration?*

Had the earthquake knocked her off that massage table and she'd hit her head? Was she hallucinating? Or in some some kind of coma?

Her and Mitch Bailey, having dinner *tête-à-tête* in the seclusion of a luxurious private villa in Bali? Maybe she'd wake up and find herself back in the spa, sprawled amid the debris with a big fat headache.

But if it *was* a dream, or a long-ago fantasy come true, she was going to enjoy every second of being with Mitch. Who knew what tomorrow might bring?

She swung her legs off the side of the lounger. 'I'll go get the room service menu.'

CHAPTER FOUR

MITCH RECLINED ON HIS lounger and watched Zoe as she walked into the living area. He couldn't keep his eyes off the way her hips swayed enticingly under the body-hugging dress. Somehow he doubted that seductive sway was intentional. He'd seen enough of the type of woman who turned on the sex appeal with seduction in mind to know the difference.

No. Zoe had a natural, unconscious sensuality. The fact that she seemed unaware of it made her only more appealing. *Zoe Summers. Who would have thought it?*

He couldn't get over the difference in her. It wasn't that he'd found her unattractive as a teenager. There'd been something quirky and rebellious about her that he'd liked. But now...now she was sexy as hell. Sparky and feisty too. He was finding it fascinating to discover the woman she'd become. Was grateful to the twist of destiny that had flung them together.

She headed back towards the pool, waving a cardboard folder. 'I had to hunt for it, but I've got the room service menu.'

Mitch swung his legs from the lounger so he sat on the edge. 'Let's take a look.'

'It's the same food as the restaurant. I've eaten there a few times. It's good.'

Menu in hand, she hesitated near his lounger. He patted the seat next to him. Cautiously she sat down, being so careful to keep a distance between them that it made him smile. Again she tugged down her dress to cover her thighs. But that only meant the neckline of her dress slid down, revealing more than a tantalising glimpse of the swell of her breasts.

Surely he would have noticed if she'd had a body like that back at school?

'What's for dinner?' he asked, shuffling a little closer to her until her scent filled his senses. 'Any recommendations?'

'I don't know what you like,' she said.

Of course she wouldn't. Despite that briefly

opened window on a shared past, he and Zoe were strangers.

'What are *you* going to order?' he asked.

'Something not too spicy,' she said. 'The curries don't agree with me.'

'Bali belly, huh?' he said. 'Happens to the best of us. But you survived?'

Zoe pulled a face. 'I'll spare you the details,' she said. 'I seem to be over it now, but don't want to risk a relapse.' She handed over the menu. 'I'm going to stick with the *ayam bakar*—I've had it before with no…uh…ill effects.'

Mitch read out the description of her chosen dish. 'Organic chicken pieces marinated in a special blend of Indonesian spices, grilled, and served with a lemongrass salsa. Sounds good.'

'It's absolutely delicious. I want to learn how to make it when I get home.'

'You like cooking?'

She nodded. 'I wanted to have cooking lessons while I was in Bali but I've run out of days.'

'Next time,' he said.

She bit her lip and paled at his words, paused

for a long moment. 'Yes,' she said finally. 'Next time.'

Mitch cursed himself for his insensitivity; he'd already suspected she was only masking her fear.

Would there be a next time? Or another earthquake? Maybe a tsunami?

Despite the manager's reassuring words Mitch knew there was a risk the entire resort would be wiped out by breakfast. But he tended towards optimism in his view of life. Not so Zoe, he suspected.

She'd lost her whole family when disaster had hit from nowhere. No wonder she was frightened. He wanted to take her in his arms and reassure her that there was a low statistical risk of any more serious danger. But he sensed she wouldn't welcome it. He sensed a 'hands off' shield around her.

'Y'know, I'm not really that hungry,' she said in a diminished voice.

She twisted her hands together. To stop them trembling, he guessed.

'You do realise it's highly unlikely anything else is going to happen?' he said gently.

Her chin rose. 'I know that.'

'There's no need to be frightened.'

'Who said I was frightened?'

'I thought that was why you'd lost your appetite?'

'No. I…' She met his gaze. 'Maybe I *am* a little frightened,' she admitted.

'Let's order for you anyway. You might get hungry later.' He scanned the menu. 'I'm hungry right now.'

'You were always hungry,' she said, with a weak smile that tugged at the corner of her mouth.

Her lovely, lovely mouth.

'Back then, I mean.'

'Your granny mightn't have been so nice, but she made good cookies.'

Zoe nodded. 'Baking cookies with her is one of the few nice memories I have of her. She liked having a boy to cook for. I realise that now.'

'Is she still around?'

Her lips tightened. 'I guess so. I don't know and I don't care.'

'I don't blame you,' he said. Not after the way she'd been treated by someone who should have cared for her. Hearing about the old woman's pregnancy fear for Zoe had given him the creeps.

She nodded and quickly changed the subject. 'Anything on the menu appeal?'

This was the first time he'd eaten at the hotel apart from breakfast. He'd spent most evenings with friends who owned the most fashionable beachfront nightclub in Seminyak. 'I'm going for the Balinese mixed seafood.'

Zoe had to shift a little closer to him to read the menu. Her scent was fresh, tangy, with an underlying sweetness. Much like her personality, he suspected.

'That looks good,' she said. 'Healthy.' She looked up at him. 'I guess you have to watch everything you eat?'

'All the time. When I'm training or before a game I carb-load. On vacation I stick with lean protein and vegetables.'

'I eat healthily too,' she said. 'But as I'm far

from a professional athlete I also make room for chocolate.'

'I can't remember when I last ate chocolate.'

From the time when he'd first started playing for Sydney soccer clubs his diet had been overseen by a nutritionist. It was all about discipline. Discipline and constant self-denial.

'You want to order dessert?' he said, flipping the menu to the appropriate page.

'Why not? The mini chocolate lava pudding with lychee ice cream might be good for my nerves.'

He liked her self-deprecating attitude to her fears. 'That's as good an excuse as any,' he said. 'Fruit salad for me. I've spent a season on the sidelines. I have to be at my peak when I start intense training again.'

She glanced at his right knee. So she knew about the incident when two opposing players had slammed into him and his anterior cruciate ligament had snapped.

'Australia's most famous knee…' she said.

Mitch found it disconcerting that Zoe was so aware of the details of his life while he knew so little about hers. He doubted he'd ever get used to the scrutiny he endured as a celebrity athlete. Even his knee had become public property.

'I wouldn't say "most *famous* knee",' he said, laughing it off.

'How about most notorious knee?' she said, her head tilted to one side, teasing.

'Notorious knee? I like that.'

Most painful knee was more like it. Both in terms of the actual injury and also in the way it had lost him a season of play. The memory of being carried off the field came flooding back. The agony. The terror that he wouldn't be able to play again. The months of rehabilitation and physiotherapy that had followed. The effort to get himself back to peak fitness after the weeks on crutches.

'I don't see a scar,' she said, her eyes narrowed.

'No scar,' he said. 'Three small incisions for keyhole surgery have left tiny marks. That's all.'

For a moment he was tempted to place Zoe's hand on his knee and let her feel the punctures. Not a good idea. He found her way too attractive to be able to trust himself.

'Is it healed now?' she asked.

'Good as new.' He wouldn't admit to anyone his niggling fear that once he was back in the game his knee would betray him again. His sporting life would be over if it did.

'There was talk that your injury might force you to retire,' she said.

'No way,' he said vehemently.

This exact injury had brought other great players' careers to a skidding halt. He wasn't going to let it end *his*.

It would take something more catastrophic than a cruciate ligament repair for his manager, his fans *or* himself to allow him to consider giving up. At the age of twenty-seven he was in his football prime. He cursed the six months it had taken him to achieve full recovery. Now he had to get back out there on the field and prove he could play better than ever.

Soccer was his life.

Zoe drew her dark brows together. 'So, why are you in Bali?'

'I was visiting family in Sydney, then decided to have a break here on the way back to Madrid.

I met up with a mate who has a surf gear business. Another runs a big nightclub.'

'When do you go back?'

'Who knows how the earthquake has affected the airlines? But I'm scheduled to fly to Singapore then back to Madrid the day after tomorrow.'

It was May. He would hurl himself into intense training immediately he got back. Pre-season games started at the end of June. He needed those 'friendly' games to test his knee and get back into top form before the season proper commenced. The first games for La Liga—the Spanish league—started at the end of August.

'What about your flight?' he asked Zoe.

'I fly out tomorrow morning, if all goes well.' She crossed her fingers.

'I guess the airlines will keep us informed,' he said.

If all goes well.

He didn't repeat her words—didn't want to bring her fear to the fore again.

There was an awkward pause that she rushed to fill. 'Do you like living in Madrid?'

'Madrid rocks. An Aussie boy from the north shore of Sydney living in one of Europe's great cities never tires.'

All true. But he hadn't admitted to anyone how lonely he could get there, despite the buzz of playing for one of the world's best teams. He had friends on the team, of course, but there were also some big egos to deal with—and the truth was they were in competition with each other as well as the opposing teams.

He wasn't about to admit to that downside now. Zoe had flitted into his life again and he was very careful of what he said to people except his family and his closest friends—careful of who he let in to his private world. You never knew who would talk to the press. Or misrepresent his words on social media. Or post a compromising selfie.

'Do you speak Spanish?' she asked.

'Enough to get by.'

Mitch decided the conversation had centred too much around him. He was way more interested in her.

'Me muero de hambre.'

Zoe laughed—a low, husky laugh that hadn't changed at all since she was a teenager. She'd grown into that sensual, adult laugh.

'You're dying of hunger. Did I get that right?'

'You speak Spanish?' He knew so little about her—wanted to know more in this accelerated getting-to-know-you situation they found themselves in.

'Hablo un poco de español,' she said, with an appropriately expressive shrug.

'You speak a little Spanish,' he translated.

'And a little French, and a little Italian, and a few phrases in Indonesian that I've learned in the last few days.'

'You've travelled a lot?'

'So far most of my travel has been of the armchair variety. I'd *like* to travel a lot. I'd love to be fluent in different languages. I'll study more some day—when I'm not so busy working.'

Of course she would. Zoe had been so smart at school. And she'd grown up into a formidable woman. Formidable and sexy. How very different from the women he usually dated. From nowhere came the thought that Zoe Summers would be a challenge. The kind of challenge it would be pleasurable to meet.

'I have no idea what work you do,' he said.

'I have my own accountancy and taxation advice company.' She paused. 'Yeah. I know. *Boring*.'

'I didn't say that,' he said.

She pulled a face. 'I can see the thought bubbles wafting around your head.' She made a series of little quote marks in the air as she sang the words in a clear contralto. '"Boring. Boring. Boring."'

He laughed. 'Wrong. My thought bubbles are "Clever Zoe" and "Intelligent" and "Entrepreneurial".'

'Oh,' she said. 'They…they're great thought bubbles.'

'But don't ask me to sing them as I'm totally tone deaf.'

She laughed. 'I'm grateful—both for the thought bubbles and for sparing me the singing.'

'You couldn't call it singing. There isn't a musical bone in my body.'

'Not a singer and not a poet?' She smiled.

'Seriously, though, my clients are anything but boring—'

'And neither are you boring,' he said.

She flushed pink, high on her cheekbones. He would have liked to trace the path of colour with his fingers, then move down to her mouth. Her lovely mouth, with the top lip slightly narrower than the bottom lip, giving it an enticing sensuality.

'That's nice,' she said simply.

'Tell me about your clients,' he said. 'I'm intrigued.'

'I specialise in working with creative people.' Her face softened. 'People like my parents, who were hopeless money-managers. Charming. Talented. My father played guitar. My mother's instrument was her voice. But they were feckless with money.'

She stopped.

'That was way more information than you wanted.'

He leaned closer to her. 'No, it wasn't. Tell me more. I'm interested in what you do.'

She backed away—so slightly he might have

thought he'd imagined it if he hadn't been so focused on her. He found it intriguing to have her nervous of him. He was used to women who were unabashed—blatant, even—in expressing their desire for him.

'Shall we order the food first, if you're so hungry?' she said, her words tumbling out in a rush. 'I know the manager said it was business as usual, but the kitchen might not be up to speed after the quake.'

Mitch's empty belly told him that was a very good idea. But he wasn't going to let her get away for long with changing the subject. He was fascinated by her—wanted to make the most of the hours they were fated to spend together.

'Okay,' he said.

She got up from the lounger. 'I'll phone it through.'

Mitch got up too, and took the menu from her. 'No. I'll order. They can bill the meal to my room.'

She went to snatch it back. 'It can be billed to my room.'

He held on firmly to the menu. When she tried

to take it he held it above his head. 'In the rar-efied space where I dwell, I pay for dinner.'

Zoe bristled at his comment. She liked to be in-dependent. 'Please at least let me pay for my own meal,' she said.

'No,' he said, in a firm, forceful way that brooked no argument.

It was a gracious gesture on his part, and it would be crass of her to argue. 'Okay. Thank you. I'll—'

She was going to say she'd pay next time, but of course it was highly unlikely she'd be having dinner again with Mitch Bailey. Further earth-quakes or not.

Mitch headed to the phone to order the meal. His back view was breathtaking: broad shoulders tapered to a swoon-worthy butt, then long, strong legs. No wonder his fans went crazy over him. Lost in admiration, she felt a tad light-headed herself.

She observed the way he walked, with the confident easy strength of a man at the peak of physical perfection. There wasn't the slightest indication that he favoured his right knee in his athletic stride. She prayed the knee was now strong enough to help him soar right back to the heights of the success he craved.

'You were right—the meal will be around an hour,' he said when he returned.

'Lucky we ordered when we did, then.'

Mitch didn't sit back down on the lounger. 'It's hot. How about cooling down in your pool?'

It *was* hot—and humid—and suddenly Zoe wanted more than anything to dive into the water. Perspiration prickled on her brow and her dress clung stickily to her back. But the pool wasn't very large. It seemed too intimate to be sharing it with him. Maybe she'd spent too long admiring his rear view. Then again, sitting outside was starting to get uncomfortable—despite the shade of the frangipani tree.

Mitch didn't hesitate. He strode to the edge of the pool and dived in with an arrow-perfect dive and barely a splash.

He swam the length of the pool underwater, his tanned, perfect body spearing through the turquoise depths. When he emerged his hair sat sleek and dark against his head, and his broad shoulders and chest glistened with drops of water caught in the late-afternoon sun. Zoe caught her breath at how handsome he looked.

'Come on in!' he called with the engaging grin that had appealed to her so much all those years ago.

Still she hesitated. Usually she wouldn't think twice about slipping off her dress and diving in. But the very act of taking off her dress in front of Mitch paralysed her. It seemed like... Well, it seemed like a striptease—as if she were displaying her body for his delectation. But it would seem ridiculous to go inside when she already had her bikini on underneath.

She compromised and turned away, angling her body for minimum exposure to Mitch. Then slid her dress up and over her head, tossing it onto the lounger.

She was aware of Mitch's gaze on her. Of the admiration in his eyes. It disconcerted her. She wasn't afraid to be seen in a bikini. She worked hard to stay slim and strong. And her fashionable bikini was quite modestly cut, in a retro style reminiscent of a swimsuit from the nine-teen-fifties.

But she was suddenly aware of how its very design drew attention to her breasts, her hips. In the past Mitch had seen her as a nerd, a geek. She doubted he'd even noticed she was female. Not with tall, curvy Lara always in tow, staking her claim on Mitch at any opportunity. Not that she'd needed to—Mitch had only had eyes for his blonde girlfriend.

But now... Now Mitch had noticed she was female. It was in his narrowed eyes, in the way his head was tilted to the side as he watched her.

And she liked it.

CHAPTER FIVE

ZOE LIKED THE way Mitch didn't hide his appreciation of the woman she'd become. She liked the easy way she could talk with him. She liked having him back in her life, even if only for these few hours. No way would she let that be ruined by feeling awkward or self-conscious. That kind of negativity had been left far behind her, in the corridors of Northside High.

He was the most beautiful man she was ever likely to meet—and not just in appearance. Scratch the surface of the mega sports star, the billboard model, the oestrogen magnet who had female hearts in a flurry all around the world, and the Mitch she'd liked so much when she was seventeen was still there. Even more confident and self-assured, but still Mitch.

Thanks to a random shifting of the tectonic plates beneath the earth's crust she'd been gifted this time before they each went back to their lives on opposite sides of the world.

She took a few swift steps to the edge of the water and waded in. Although a more than competent swimmer, she didn't want to risk an embarrassing belly flop in front of one of the world's elite athletes.

Zoe gasped and squealed at the initial coolness of the water, then welcomed it. With slow, easy strokes she swam from one end of the pool to the other. On her return lap she found herself very close to Mitch—so close their bodies actually nudged in the water: thigh against thigh, hip against hip. His body was strong, hard, muscular.

A shiver of pleasure ran through her at the contact. Had he noticed? Hastily she pushed away through the water to swim another lap.

He must be so used to women fawning all over him. That would *not* be her. She was determined to seem friendly, but not too friendly. No groupie-like grasping for attention from Mr Sexiest Man Alive for her. Much as she might yearn for it.

Her laps completed, she stood facing him in the shallow end of the pool, the water up to her waist

'That was a good idea. So refreshing.'

'It's not a huge pool, but it works,' he said.

No doubt he was staying in one of the larger, more luxurious villas the size of a house at the other end of the resort.

'This pool's only meant for two,' she said, breathless more from her proximity to him than from the vigour of her swimming. 'These villas are popular with honeymooners, I believe.'

She was suddenly heart-stoppingly aware of the utter privacy afforded by the high wall and the tropical trees and shrubs that grew above it, the solid, ornately carved wooden gate. A couple could frolic without a stitch on in this pool and no one would know.

'I booked in to this place because I wanted privacy,' Mitch said. He looked down to the bare third finger of her left hand. 'Why are you here on your own?'

'Because I want to be,' she said, careful to keep her voice matter-of-fact. 'May is a good time to take a break before all the end-of-financial-year mayhem in the final weeks of June.'

No need to mention that she'd needed to get away on her own to escape the fallout of a relationship break-up.

'That wasn't what I meant,' Mitch said with a slow grin. 'I wanted to know if there was a man in your life.'

'Oh,' she said. It was a reasonable question but she felt flustered by it. As if he'd been reading her mind. 'No,' she said. 'Not...not any more.'

'That surprises me,' he said.

She was aware of his appreciative gaze taking in the swell of her breasts over the top of her bikini bra, her bare shoulders and arms. She sucked in her stomach.

'There was someone. But...but I broke up with him a month ago.'

'Were you meant to come here with him?' He gestured around him. 'To this "couples' paradise"?'

'We were talking about Thailand. This was a last-minute booking.'

He nodded. 'Yeah, you said.' Mitch's green

eyes narrowed. 'So you came to Bali to nurse a broken heart?'

'No.' She sighed, looked down at the water where it rippled around them. 'More likely I...I broke *his* heart.'

'I didn't take you for the heartbreaker type,' Mitch said.

Zoe slowly shook her head. 'I didn't think I was the heartbreaker type either. I've had my share of dating hurt, but it's not pleasant to be the one dishing it out. I'm not proud of it. He was a wonderful guy.'

'But not wonderful enough to go on vacation with?'

She met his gaze. 'Not wonderful enough to marry. We were talking about taking a vacation together. Then he turned it around to talk of a honeymoon.'

'And you ran scared?' Mitch said.

'I don't know about being scared. I just didn't feel the same way he did.'

She was beginning to wonder if there was something wrong with her that at the age of twenty-seven she still didn't want to commit to a man. This recent proposal was the second one she'd turned down. But she wasn't going to share that with Mitch.

'You're not interested in marriage?' he asked.

'Of course I am. One day. And I'd like to have a family. But not now. Not to him—nice as he was. I didn't feel strongly enough to make that kind of commitment.'

The conversation was taking on a more personal slant than she cared for. But the shock of the earthquake, the surprise of seeing Mitch again, had loosened her inhibitions about talking about her love-life—or lack of it.

'Fair enough,' he said.

'I won't compromise. When I get married it will be because I'm head over heels in love and know it will last for ever.'

His brow raised. 'Okay...'

She laughed. 'You're looking at me as if you can't believe I said that.'

'I was surprised,' he admitted. 'I took you more for the practical, pragmatic type.'

'Because I'm an accountant with a business degree?'

'Who knew that underneath the number-crunching and the bean-counting there beats the heart of a romantic?'

Zoe tried not to sound defensive. 'Maybe it *is* ridiculously romantic of me, but I want the kind of love my parents had. They adored each other. I won't settle for less.'

'Admirable,' he said.

'But over-idealistic?'

'I didn't say that.'

'Just raised your eyebrows and let me think it?'

He grinned. 'I didn't realise my eyebrows were so expressive.

'You'd be surprised what your eyebrows reveal about you,' she said.

Mitch waggled his eyebrows. 'What are my eyebrows saying now?'

Zoe paused to think up a sassy reply—only to be hit by a splash of expertly aimed pool water.

'Hey!' she spluttered, wiping water from her eyes with the back of her hand. 'What was that for?'

His eyes crinkled in amusement. 'You didn't

read my eyebrows quickly enough, did you? They were challenging you to a water fight.'

'Challenge accepted,' she said without further hesitation. 'This is war.'

Laughing, she angled around him, shooting sprays of water with the edge of her hand as she struck the surface. Laughing too, he retaliated faster, harder, until the spray was constant between them. Defence became attack; attack became defence.

As Mitch pulled his arm way back, for a powerful splash she couldn't hope to deflect, Zoe ducked and swam underwater to the other end of the pool before resurfacing.

'Hah! Retreating from the battlefield,' said Mitch.

'A tactical move to regroup my energies,' Zoe said breathless, laughing, pushing back her wet hair from her eyes.

Mitch raised his hands above his head. 'I surrender,' he said, with that big, endearing grin that had made him the darling of the women's magazines.

It wouldn't take much for her to surrender to him.

With just a few strokes of his strong, sinewy arms he had reached her. He wasn't the slightest bit out of breath.

'Why don't I trust that surrender one little bit?' she said, moving back in the water so she could feel the edge of the pool at her spine.

'Because I learned the game fighting dirty with my three brothers in our backyard pool,' he said, stopping just a pace from her.

'Let's call it a draw, then, shall we?' she said. Her heart was pounding—not from exertion, but from his closeness: the muscled breadth of his chest, the washboard abs.

The utter male perfection of him.

'I'm a competitive guy. I don't give in too easily.'

She didn't know whether the towering conquest in his stance was real or part of the game. Her heartbeat skipped up a further gear.

She met his gaze for a long moment before replying. 'I'm a diplomatic woman. I'm thinking of ways we can end this peacefully.'

Oh, she could think of several ways that she'd never dare put voice to.

He laughed. 'Seriously? How can I argue against that? I really am conceding.'

'Can I trust you?' she asked playfully.

He held out his hands, palms up in supplication. 'You can trust me, Zoe,' he said.

Other words unspoken hung in the air. Trust had been an issue in their brief, shared past. But he had redeemed himself by apologising for the incident that had ended their youthful friendship.

This was just a game.

The silence was broken by the loud crowing of a rooster coming from a few buildings away.

'The final word comes from Mr Rooster,' Zoe said.

Mitch scowled. 'Darn bird. He crows morning, noon and night.'

'He must have quite the harem of hens to keep happy.'

'It's not a sound I hear in the heart of old Madrid.'

'Or me in Balmain, in inner Sydney.'

'You live in Balmain?'

She nodded. 'In a converted warehouse on the waterfront, overlooking Mort Bay.'

'I played the Balmain Tigers in junior club. They were a good team. Beat 'em, of course.'

'You really are competitive, aren't you?'

'Only winners are grinners,' he said, and although he was smiling his words rang true. 'In my game you can't afford to be anything else.'

'An attacking midfielder. That's what I've seen you described as. It sounds aggressive.'

Zoe had seen him play on screen: swift, superbly balanced, relentless and graceful all at the same time. No other player had caught her attention. She'd thrilled at the TV commentator's praise for Mitch. While she didn't know a lot about soccer, she'd got what the commentator had meant when he'd said Mitch had the vision to split a defence with unerringly accurate passes perfectly weighted to gift his teammates with scoring opportunities. No wonder his team wanted him back.

His jaw set. 'You have to be aggressive to win, Zoe. Tactical and ruthless.'

'And you're all about winning?'

'The game is *everything*.' He emphasised the word so there was no missing his message.

'And in your personal life?'

'What personal life?' he joked, but his eyes were shadowed and serious.

He had quizzed her about *her* love-life; she had a few questions of her own.

'You were with Lara for a long time,' she said.

Again, she didn't want him to think she'd been stalking him. But Mitch's hometown girl-friend had attracted lots of media attention—both in Australia and overseas. Lara had only got blonder and more glamorous as she'd grown up. The golden couple had been all over the media, and Lara had become the queen bee of the contingent of footballers' wives and girlfriends the media nicknamed WAGs.

'We had our ups and downs,' Mitch muttered.

Zoe wouldn't have been human if she hadn't felt a small degree of satisfaction when she'd seen Mitch had finally split with Lara. Much as she'd put that incident at school behind her, Lara's maliciousness had been impossible to forget. She'd been the meanest of the mean girls. *Mitch deserved better.*

'I'm sorry,' she said, willing her voice to sound sincere.

Mitch shrugged and water slicked off his broad shoulders. 'Don't be. We broke up and got back together so many times. It was never going to work.'

From his carefully schooled expression and even tone of voice Zoe sensed there was more to it than Mitch was saying. That was okay. It was none of her business.

'No one special since?' She thought of the parade of Lara look-alikes who'd featured briefly on Mitch's arm.

He turned to scoop up a palm frond that had fallen into the water and tossed it out onto the courtyard, his back rippling with sculpted muscle. 'I don't have time for someone special. Date someone more than a few times and they start thinking it's more than a casual thing.'

Who could blame the poor girls for wanting more with a man like Mitch?

'You must get women flinging themselves at

you all the time.' *But what a way to get your heart broken.*

He shifted and looked uncomfortable. 'Football groupies and over-eager fans come with the territory,' he said. 'What's more difficult is meeting genuine women not blinded by money and fame.'

'I can see that, but—'

He cut across her. 'But that's irrelevant right now. My personal life is on hold. Indefinitely. I've got something to prove. There's no room in my life for relationships. Not now. Not for years.'

'You're focusing on success and nothing is going to distract you?'

'That's exactly right,' he said. 'I'm glad you understand. Women usually think they can change my mind.'

'The hopes of all those fans shattered!' she said with mock mournfulness.

'And you breaking hearts all the way, let me remind you.'

'If you put it like that...'

'Putting it like that makes us both single,' he said, his deep voice a tone deeper.

'Yes,' she murmured through a suddenly choked throat.

For a long, still moment their eyes held. The intensity of his gaze reminded her of Mitch as a student, determined to understand the subject she was helping him to master. Back then he'd been reading a page in a poetry book; right now it felt as if he was reading her face as his gaze searched her eyes, her mouth.

In turn she explored *his* face. His chiselled face. His strong jaw. The knowing glint in his green eyes framed by those too-expressive eyebrows. And his mouth, lifted to a half-smile that gave a promise of pleasure that made her own lips part in anticipation, her breath quicken.

Her eyes locked with his and a thrill of anticipation tingled through her.

Mitch Bailey was about to kiss her. And she was going to kiss him right back.

CHAPTER SIX

MITCH HAD BEEN aching to kiss Zoe ever since she'd joined him in the pool. But just as his lips grazed hers, just as her lips parted under his, just as she uttered a delicious little moan of surprise and need, an Oriental-sounding chime came from the carved gate to the villa.

'Room service!' called a cheerful voice with a lilting Balinese accent.

Mitch stilled. Zoe looked up into his eyes. He saw echoed in hers the same frustration he was feeling at being thwarted in their first kiss.

For a long moment they stood motionless in the water, his mouth still claiming hers, her hands resting on his shoulders in silent agreement to pretend they weren't there.

The doorbell chimed again.

Mitch muttered a curse under his breath. Then he pulled Zoe closer and kissed her hard. She wound her arms around his neck and kissed him back with equal passion. Heat ignited between them so fast he was surprised steam wasn't rising from the water.

Damn the room service timing.

With regret he let her go, then pulled her back for a final swift kiss. If she could see his thought bubble now it would give her the promise torn from him. *Later.*

'Come in,' he called to the waiter on the other side of the gate, his voice hoarse.

Reluctantly he let Zoe go, supporting her when she seemed to stagger in the water. When she'd regained her balance he swam to the edge of the pool, then turned back to check she was okay.

The sight of her wading out of the water made him suck in a gasp of admiration. *She was awesome.* With both hands she pushed her wet hair from her face, so it was slicked behind her ears and flat to her head. The severe hairstyle emphasised the angular, unconventional beauty of her face. That black bikini concealed more than it revealed, yet he found the very subtlety of it tantalising. Zoe was smart, fun, *different*. He couldn't remember when he'd last bantered and laughed like that with a woman.

He flung a blue-striped beach towel around his shoulders and handed her one as she got out of the pool. 'It's an improvement on the white one,' he said in a low voice.

'Anything would be an improvement on that,' she said, her voice not quite steady as she wrapped the towel around her.

The smiling young waiter, dressed in the version of traditional garb that formed the staff's uniform, carried in a large silver tray. He placed the tray on the outdoor table and, with a flourish, lifted the lids that covered the plates.

'*Terima kasih*—thank you,' Zoe said to the waiter with her vibrant smile.

Her teeth were perfect—even and white. Had she worn braces at school? Mitch couldn't be sure. He was racking his brains to try and remember everything about her back then.

Their dinner was presented with simple Asian elegance. No one would know it had come from a kitchen suffering the after-effects of an earthquake. Deliciously spicy smells wafted from the tray and Mitch's stomach rumbled. But hunger of a different kind was foremost in his mind.

He echoed Zoe's thanks to the waiter, tipped him generously, and watched impatiently for the high, ornate gate to close behind him.

Finally he was alone again with Zoe, in the total privacy of the villa. It seemed suddenly very quiet. He was aware of the faint lapping of the water against the sides of the pool; the rustle of birds settling for the night in the surrounding trees. He swore he could even hear the fizzing of the bubbles in the mineral water Zoe had ordered. A faint smell of incense wafted across from the nearby Hindu temple, to mingle with the aromas of their dinner and the sweetness of frangipani blossom.

Mitch found he had to clear his throat to speak. 'Dinner is served,' he said, with a mock bow.

'So I see. It smells amazing. I...I'm suddenly hungry again.'

There was an edge to her voice—as if she were trying too hard to make conversation. She tugged at the knot that kept the beach towel secure between her breasts.

'The waiter has gone,' he said. 'You can ditch the towel.'

'I'd rather keep it on,' she said.

'Because it's so cold?'

Although it was starting to get dark, it was still hot, the air thick and humid.

'I feel more comfortable covered up,' she said, not meeting his eyes.

'Zoe—'

'Mitch—' she said at the same time.

'Back then—'

'In…in the pool—' she stuttered.

'When we—'

She raised her eyes to meet his. 'I don't think it should happen again. The…the kiss, I mean.'

'I didn't think you meant the water fight,' Mitch quipped.

She smiled and her shoulders visibly relaxed. 'I enjoyed the water fight.' She flushed high on her cheekbones. 'I…I enjoyed the kiss.'

'I'm glad to hear that.' He couldn't keep the irony from his tone.

'But…'

With a sinking feeling, Mitch had known there was a *but* coming.

'But, considering the circumstances, I think we should stick to…to being friends.'

Mitch felt intense disappointment with an overlay of relief. He suspected Zoe wasn't the kind of girl for a one-night fling. And right now that was all he could offer with his life the way it was. He'd hurt her in the past. He certainly had no wish to hurt her now.

'You're right,' he said through gritted teeth.

Of course she was right—much as he might wish otherwise, much as he ached for her to continue that kiss.

'Just friends.'

'Thank you,' she murmured.

But he wanted her.

This urgent desire for her had come from left field. He hadn't looked at Zoe in that way when they'd been teenagers, much as he'd liked her. He'd been with Lara, and he'd prided himself on being faithful even then.

But now he was single, and the sway of Zoe's hips, the swell of her breasts, her lovely mouth and her husky laughter was driving him crazy with want. However, he knew it would be better for her if he held back and didn't act on that desire. Better for him too. He didn't want to carry another burden of guilt away with him when they said goodbye.

'So we'll treat that kiss as the spoils of our water battle in the swimming pool?' he said, forcing his voice to sound light-hearted.

'In which both sides triumphed,' she said, with a sigh that sounded halfway between relief and regret. Which only made him want her more.

Oh, yes, a kiss from Mitch was a prize indeed.

Zoe's head was still spinning from the impact of Mitch's brief but passionate possession of her mouth. His lips had only been on hers for such a short time, but the joy of it had been seared into her soul.

If a kiss felt like that what would making love with him be like?

She pushed the thought far, far away into the deepest recesses of her heart.

Had she always wanted this? Her body pulled close to his? The taste of him? the touch of him? The sheer bliss of being with him?

That teenage crush had never gone away.

It was only one kiss. But it had awakened a desire for him so powerful it would have led to more than a kiss. And she couldn't deal with that. Not when he'd made it so clear that there was no room for a woman in his life. Not when, once this brief alignment of their planets was over, they'd go back to their different worlds. *She would probably never see him again.* Her desire for him was as impossible as that deeply buried crush had been so long ago.

'No need to look so woeful,' he said.

He pulled her into a hug. She hesitated at first, then relaxed into his arms. Her head rested on his shoulder and he stroked her hair. She closed her eyes, the better to savour the utter pleasure of his hands on her.

'It's not our time, not our place,' he said. 'But I'm glad we met up again, Zoe Summers. I'm pleased to count you as a friend.'

'Me too,' she said, wishing she could stay in his arms longer, knowing it wasn't a good idea. Her in a bikini, him in his swim shorts—full-body, bare skin contact. While her mind was telling her to pull away her body was clamouring for more.

'Let's enjoy our dinner,' he said. 'Then I'll go back to my villa. Because I can't guarantee I won't kiss you again.'

Zoe blinked down hard on a sudden smarting of tears. 'Good idea. I…I mean bad idea. I mean *wise* idea.'

She pulled away from his hug, feeling bereft of his warmth, his strength, and forced her voice to sound cheerful and matter-of-fact when inside she was a churning mess of conflict.

It would be only too easy to tell him to stay. But then, when they went their separate ways, she would have to live with it—and that might throw her right back into those high school feelings of unworthiness she'd worked so hard to shake off. Her life was settled, steady, sure—dull compared to his.

She could never be part of Mitch's world.

She tucked the beach towel around her a little more firmly. *'Usted debe ser hambre,'* she said in her best Spanish accent.

'Now that you mention it, yes, I am starving,'

he said. He took her hand and led her to where the waiter had set up their dinner table, with two chairs facing opposite each other. 'Let's make the most of this meal.'

Zoe did her best. The *ayam bakar* with lemongrass salsa was one of the best chicken dishes Zoe had ever enjoyed. But she managed only a few half-hearted bites, pushing it around her plate. Mitch, on the contrary, ate heartily. By not eating was she trying to postpone the moment dinner was over? If so, what did that mean *he* was doing?

He pushed his plate away with a satisfied sigh. 'The food in Madrid is amazing, but this fish is up there with the best meal ever.'

'It looked really good,' she said, struggling to make polite conversation.

'But you've hardly touched yours,' he said.

'I'm not really hungry,' she murmured, the knot in her stomach tightening.

'Why don't we wait a while before we eat dessert?' he said.

'Good idea,' she said.

Anything to postpone the time when they had to say goodbye.

Darkness had fallen, but the sensor-driven lights hidden in the greenery and at the edge of the pool had been switched on. The scene was peaceful and beautiful.

'This time last night I was watching the sunset on the beach,' Mitch said.

'Me too,' she said.

She wished he hadn't evoked the memory of it. Standing on the endless stretch of the dark Seminyak sand, watching the magnificence of the sun sinking into the sea, had been the only times she'd felt lonely on this solitary vacation. To know Mitch had been somewhere on the same beach somehow made it worse.

He got up from his chair.

'Let's sit over here,' he said, heading towards the loungers.

He dragged away the small table from in between and pushed the loungers together. When he'd sat down he patted the lounger next to him. It was an invitation she could not resist.

Mitch put a friendly arm around her. She relaxed against his shoulder, breathing in the clean, male scent of him, storing up the memory of it to relive next time she saw him on television, playing the game he loved so much on some international soccer pitch, where tens of thousands of spectators watched him in the flesh.

How would she be able to bear it?

At that precise moment the rooster chose the occasion for another of his raucous, triumphant cries, which lifted her from her maudlin thoughts.

'Trust him to have the last word,' she said.

Both she and Mitch laughed.

But the laughter froze in her throat as she noticed the still turquoise surface of the swimming pool start to shimmer—as if a giant hand had picked up the concrete edge and shaken it.

CHAPTER SEVEN

LAUGHING AND FOOLING AROUND with Mitch had distracted Zoe from the danger of a possible aftershock. Now her fear came rushing back as powerfully as a possible tsunami.

The loungers she and Mitch were reclining on started to shake. The plates, knives and forks and glasses from their unfinished feast clattered together. Zoe shrank against Mitch, paralysed with terror. The whimpering that echoed in her ears came from her.

'Under the table—now,' Mitch urged, and he helped her roll off the lounger and crawl to the table. He pushed her under first, then squeezed in with her, putting his arm around her to pull her tight to him.

Was this it—the big one?

Every so often she had nightmares about being in the car when the truck had hit them. Of struggling in and out of consciousness with

an agonising pain in her leg. Paramedics talking to her in soothing tones with an edge of pity
they hadn't been able to suppress. No one an-
swering her questions about her parents. The
eventual dreadful knowledge that she would
never see them again.

She was usually successful at pushing thoughts
of her loss to the dark shadows at the back of her
mind. Not so now.

Earlier today something with the potential to
wipe out her world had again come from nowhere, completely out of her control. Now it was
threatening her again.

She burrowed her face against Mitch's shoulder, grateful for his comfort, his strength, for the
soothing reassuring sounds he was making as he
stroked her back.

'You'll be okay. I think it's only a tiny tremor,'
he repeated.

As it happened, he was right. It was probably only seconds rather than minutes before the
tremor subsided.

For a few long moments she stayed in Mitch's
protective embrace as the resort settled again.

'Do you think there'll be another tremor?' she asked, her voice muffled.

'Difficult to say,' he said. 'If anything catastrophic had happened—like a tsunami warning—we would have heard alarms by now.'

'That...that wasn't too bad.' She lifted her head to meet his gaze but was reluctant to move out of the comforting circle of his arms, the illusion of safety under the table.

'I think it's safe to come out now,' he said with that disarming smile, but he made no effort to move away from her.

'Thank you,' she said, mildly ashamed of her reaction. 'I never thought I'd dive under a table twice in one day.'

She'd always prided herself on her level-headedness. *But she had been afraid.*

She eased away from his arms and crawled out from under the table while Mitch did the same, then stood next to him as they looked around them. Except for a further scattering of frangipani blossoms and a new palm frond on the surface of the pool, now still again, there had been no damage. The rooster was going crazy—but then he did tend to sound off at this time of evening.

But what if it hadn't been that way?

What if she and Mitch had been injured? What if she'd never seen him again not because he'd gone back to Madrid but because he...?

She couldn't bear even to think through the rest.

Or what if another quake came during the night and...?

You could never be certain of tomorrow.

'You okay?' he said.

She nodded. 'You?'

'Fine. It was nothing compared to the last one. Though it did jolt me.'

'I'm glad you didn't go back to your villa.'

'Me too,' he said. 'I would have been in a state without you to hold on to.'

He was being kind, uttering the self-deprecating words for her sake. She knew that. It was she who had fallen to pieces. Not him. He hadn't been afraid. Not for a moment. He was just trying to make her feel better.

That seemed to be Mitch all round. Sexiest

man alive. Star athlete. Fun. And kind. In short, the most wonderful man she had ever met or was ever likely to meet. *Mitch was unique.* And not just because of the way he looked or his skill with a ball.

The earthquake had dropped him into her life again and shaken the way she thought to its very foundations. Nothing could be the same.

Suddenly everything became very clear. She did not want to be plagued with regrets. This might be the only chance she ever had to be with Mitch.

She couldn't let him go back to his villa.

She turned to face him and clutched his arm so hard he winced. Her heart was thudding so loudly she was surprised he couldn't hear it, and her mouth was dry.

'Don't go tonight, Mitch. Stay with me.'

His eyes seemed to darken to a deeper shade of green. 'Zoe, are you sure?'

She tilted her face to his, twined her arms around his neck and kissed him. He seemed surprised, and paused for just a second before he kissed her back. His lips were warm and firm and exciting beneath hers and she explored the way he tasted, the way he felt. Mitch hugged her to him as he deepened the kiss so it escalated into a passionate meeting of mouths, tongues, teeth.

Desire for him rushed through her—urgent, demanding, insistent. *She wanted him and she wanted him now.*

It wasn't about the earthquake—that was just a facilitator. It was about *him.* If she'd bumped into him at sunset on the beach she would have wanted him. If she'd chanced upon him in a bar in Seminyak and they'd got chatting she would have wanted him.

She was realistic. Mitch obviously went for stunningly beautiful girls like Lara—blonde and glamorous. She, Zoe, hitting average on the looks scale, was never likely to capture Mitch Bailey's attention. But here, now, she had.

She'd wanted him at seventeen and hadn't been able to have him. Now she was going to take what she wanted. Even if it was for only one night.

She broke the kiss and pulled away, panting and breathless. 'I...I think we should go inside.'

'It's completely private here—look at the height of those walls.'

'Wh…what about helicopters?'

Mitch's brow rose, bemused. 'Helicopters? Why would you worry about *helicopters*?'

She felt a little foolish. 'I don't know. Your world is so different to mine. But I thought—'

Mitch laughed, but it was laughter free of mockery. 'I'm not so famous that I'm harassed by paparazzi buzzing overhead in helicopters.'

'Just being sure,' she said. 'I would hate to see a blurry photo of us on the internet, with a reference to myself as the "mystery brunette" seen making out with Mitch Bailey in his luxurious Bali villa.'

'Not going to happen,' he said.

'You're sure of that?' she said, with more than a touch of worry.

Mitch trailed a finger along the curve of her jaw, sending a jolt of awareness through every pleasure receptor in her body. 'What happens in your villa stays in your villa,' he said. 'I don't want publicity either.'

'I'd still be happier if we went inside,' she said.

The walls were high, but she *would* prefer to be behind closed doors with Mitch, safe from any curious eyes.

'Just one thing before we go,' he said.

He picked up a frangipani blossom and tucked in behind her ear, making it a caress.

The gesture undid her. Who knew Mitch could be so romantic?

'Thank you,' she said with a slow smile. 'I love the scent.'

'And a second thing…'

He reached over and undid the knot that secured her beach towel so it fell to the ground.

Zoe in his arms. Zoe kissing him. Zoe wanting him to stay with her.

There was nothing he wanted more.

But, much as he ached to pick her up and carry her into her bedroom, Mitch knew he had to slow things down.

For all Zoe's sassiness and smarts, Mitch sensed a vulnerability about her that had not lessened since he'd known her as a recently bereaved seventeen-year-old. The foundations of her life had been yanked out from underneath her. This earthquake had shaken them some more—and he didn't just mean literally.

He wanted to take up her invitation. But he wanted her to be sure what she was letting herself in for. He could not damage her further.

As soon as they got inside the villa Zoe tilted her face to his. Her flawless skin was flushed, her brown eyes luminous with desire, and her lips were parted on a half-smile that was so seductive he caught his breath. Laughing that low, husky laugh, as though she knew her power over him, she pulled him to her for another urgent kiss.

When the kiss threatened to get out of control he broke away, smoothed her hair—drying now into a dark mass of waves—from around from her face, and secured the flower behind her ear. He liked the way it looked there—exotic, sensual. Then he cupped her face in his hands, looked deep into her eyes.

He had to clear his throat to speak. 'Before we go any further we have to be sure. This is all there can be for us. Tonight.'

She laughed a husky, strangled laugh. 'Tonight might be all we ever have. We could wake up to find ourselves floating out to sea.'

'There's that,' he said. 'But—'

She put a finger to his lips to silence him.

He moved it away, then slipped his fingers through hers and firmly held her hand by her side.

'This has to be said.'

He was trying to be the sensible one here, when all he could think of was how much he wanted Zoe.

She made a pretend pout, which astounded him, and had him fighting the temptation to kiss her again.

'I don't want to waste any more time talking,' she murmured.

He groaned. Did she know what she was doing to him? He gave in to temptation and planted a quick kiss on her lovely mouth. But that was it until they'd got this sorted. He wanted her—but he did not want her hurt.

'You're amazing, Zoe. Gorgeous. Fun. Smart as ever. A surprise. But there's no room for a serious relationship in my life. Not for years. Not until I'm thirty. Maybe thirty-five. I was at the top of my game when I got injured. I have to prove myself all over again. I can't afford… emotional entanglements.'

She shook her head and made a little murmur of impatience. 'Can't you see I'm not looking beyond tonight? The world as we know it could be wiped out—I want to take the chance for us to be together while we can. You were wonderful when you were a teenager and you've grown into a wonderful man. All the qualities you had then are still there, and more. I want to spend this night with you. No matter what tomorrow might bring.'

'Thank you,' he said, moved by her words.

Back then, he realised, she had seen potential in him that others hadn't; only Zoe had recognised him as more than a good-looking jock.

'I could say the same about you.'

There was a wistful edge to her smile. 'Thank you. But, as I said earlier, we live on different planets. I'm not expecting more from you than this one night.'

He started to say something but she put her finger across his mouth again.

'I want you. But I wouldn't want a relationship with someone in the public eye—a man who belongs to his fans, not one hundred per cent to me. I'd be miserable with someone who travels the world while I'm left at home, torturing myself with thoughts about the women who might be throwing themselves at him. I'm a private person. I don't want the world to know me because of the man I'm with. I…I could never be a WAG.'

Though her words made absolute sense, he found them more than a touch insulting. That *was* his life. And it was the best life a guy could have. *It was all he wanted.* For him it wasn't about the kudos, the fame, the money. It was about the game.

'That's a lot about what you *don't* want,' he said. 'Now let's hear what you *do* want, Zoe.'

She pulled one of those faces he found so appealing. 'We've established it's ridiculously romantic of me, but one day I want a real, for ever kind of love.'

'Like your parents had?'

She nodded. 'Not just for me, but for my children. I had the happiest childhood you can imagine. It was erratic. We moved from one shared household to another. From one failed venture to another. And at the age of ten I knew how to lie to a debt collector. But I was secure in the love my parents had for each other and for me. I want to love and be loved on that scale. I…I think I value it so much because it was wrenched away from me.'

'And that happened not long before I first knew you.' He felt a surge of anger against his younger self, who had hurt her at a time when she hadn't needed more hurt added to her burden.

'When you first knew me I was like a…like a creature who had been wrenched from its cocoon way too soon and thrown into the harsh reality of life with a grandmother who resented me.'

Mitch realised his parents also had a good marriage. They argued. There was noise and fireworks. But they were happy, and they'd raised well-balanced, successful sons. It was a fine goal to aspire to. *Just not yet.* Marriage right now would seem like a trap.

'I guess that's what I want too, one day. But not now.'

He'd made a lot of sacrifices to get where he was. Since he'd left school he hadn't had what most people would call a 'normal' life. Giving up any thought of a permanent relationship was another sacrifice he was more than happy to make. But if he could have Zoe for tonight—for one night—that would be something very special.

She looked up to him. 'Mitch, you asked me what I really want…'

'Yes. And you told me.'

'I told you what I want for the future. Ask me what I want for *now*.'

'I'm asking you,' he said, his voice hoarse with need.

Her eyes were huge and her mouth quivered. 'I want *you*, Mitch. Just you.'

He could not resist her any longer.

With a groan, he lifted her up to sit on the edge of the countertop. She wound her arms around his neck, her thighs gripping his waist as he held her to him. He kissed her mouth, deep and demanding, then pressed urgent, hungry kisses down the smooth column of her throat as she arched her body to his.

He hoped his kisses would transmit everything he couldn't say about how glad he was to be with her on this night, when they didn't know what they might wake up to the next hour, the next day. He kissed her and kissed her and kissed her—until kissing was no longer enough.

Zoe was woken by the soft, insistent buzzing of her mobile phone to let her know there was a text message for her.

For a moment she didn't know where she was. She blinked against the early-morning light filtering in through the louvered doors. Heard that noisy rooster greeting the dawn.

She was in Bali. Still alive. With Mitch.

Mitch.

He lay beside her on his back, the sheets rumpled around his hips, his arms flung above his head in total relaxation. Her breath caught at how beautiful he was. *Beautiful* wasn't a word she'd normally use to describe a man, but it fitted Mitch. His smooth skin was gilded by the sunlight, his face rough with golden stubble she wanted to reach over and stroke. But she didn't want to risk waking him.

Her heart gave a huge, painful lurch at the thought that she would most likely never see him again. But if she'd woken up alone this morning she would have always regretted it.

Cautiously, so as not to disturb him, she reached over to her phone and slid the buzzer off. It was a message from the airline. Her plane back to Sydney was on schedule. She needed to be at the airport in two hours. That just gave her time to have breakfast with Mitch. To say goodbye.

No.

She couldn't bear that.

This kind of situation was a first for her. She could only imagine how awkward and embarrassing it would be to face him. Last night with Mitch had been perfect. She wanted to keep its perfection encapsulated in her mind for ever. Not sullied by awkward goodbyes, murmured promises they both knew would never be fulfilled.

Besides, she rationalised, the Ngurah Rai International Airport at Denpasar was sure to be bedlam because of the earthquake and its aftershock. She wanted to make sure she got on that plane and out of here; she didn't think she could cope with another tremor.

She looked back at Mitch, breathing deeply and evenly in her bed. They'd both got what they'd needed from each other at a time of threat and uncertainty. Comfort. Reassurance. *Sex*.

Oh, yes. Sex such as she'd never imagined. Sex that had seen her soaring to unimaginable heights of pleasure with Mitch. Again and again. Then again, when they'd woken some time after midnight, turned into each other's arms, laughed at the fact that they could still want each other after all the satisfaction they'd already given each other, and once more made love.

Afterwards they'd crept outside to the courtyard in the moonlight and polished off their abandoned desserts—even her melted ice cream—whispering and stifling their laughter when Mitch had threatened to crow out loud like a rooster.

They'd finally gone to sleep entwined in each other's arms.

Now, she supported herself on her elbow as she admired him for the last time—his handsome face, his finely honed athlete's body. In repose, his features looked much as when she'd first met him as a teenager, but layered now with the strength and character of a successful man.

For a fleeting, heart-wrenching moment she wished that things could be different.

She could so easily fall in love with Mitch.

She acknowledged the thought before she pummelled it, vanquished it, shoved it away into the furthest corner of her heart, never to be acknowledged again.

She slid out from the sheets as silently as she could. Mitch murmured in his sleep, threw out an arm across her abandoned pillow. She stilled. Held her breath. Waited a heartbeat, then another. But he didn't wake up.

She crept to the bathroom, then haphazardly flung her stuff into the wheeled carry-on bag that was her only luggage. She regretted the lack of the batik bikini; she should have bought it when she saw it. She tugged a brush through her hair… decided to put on her make-up at the airport.

As quietly as she could she checked the closet, the bathroom, the hooks behind the bathroom door for anything she might have left behind. Before she slid on her shoes she tiptoed into the bedroom for a final silent farewell to the special man who had brought her body alive with so much pleasure last night.

She could not resist bringing her face to his and pressing a butterfly-light kiss on his beard-roughened cheek.

'Thank you,' she whispered.

Her heart caught at his sleepy murmur in response, at his faint smile. But he was still asleep.

She filled her memories with one final look at him. Then she turned and walked out through her hotel room, past the still waters of the pool, where three pink frangipani blossoms floated on the surface, and through the ornately carved wooden gate that led to the outside without looking back.

* * *

Mitch woke to bright sunlight that made him screw his eyes up against it. *Zoe.* Memories of the night he'd spent with her came flooding back.

'Stay with me,' he murmured, still half asleep.

He rolled over, seeking her, wanting to pull her close. He could smell her scent on his pillow, on *him.* But he was alone in Zoe's king-size hotel bed, the sheets next to him crumpled and cold.

Fully awake now, he strained to hear if she was in the shower. But the door to the adjoining bathroom was open and no one was in there.

'Zoe?' he called.

He swung himself out of the bed.

'Are you there?' His voice echoed in the empty stillness of the room.

Then he noticed the closet door, ajar so he could see where a row of empty hangers swung. A drawer had been left slightly open.

Naked, he padded out into the living area. He looked through the sliding glass doors to the empty pool area. Plates and glasses lay haphazardly on the round table where they'd left them after their post-midnight snack.

Then he noticed the stack of Indonesian rupiah near the telephone. *'For the maid—thank you,'* was written in a bold, slanted hand on a piece of hotel notepaper.

She was gone.

He sank onto the sofa, stabbed by a feeling he couldn't put a name to. Loss. Regret. *Loneliness.*

The pain of it made him double over, his elbows on his knees, his head cradled in his hands. *Zoe.* What an amazing woman. Last night had been like nothing he'd ever experienced before. Her lithe, slender body. Her generous mouth. Her laughter. Her warmth. Her wit. The thoughtfulness and tenderness that was innate to her.

Zoe.

He wanted to roar out her name so she could hear him wherever she was—at the airport, on the plane. Hear him and come back to him.

But that couldn't be.

He had a difficult road ahead of him. Starting over. Fighting for his place in every game. Proving to the naysayers that his knee injury had not relegated him to the status of a once great player.

He could not be distracted by a woman. And

Zoe would be a major distraction. She was a for ever kind of woman—and for ever was a long way away from him. She deserved more than what he had to give.

The game. *The Beautiful Game.* That was the important thing.

A woman he could love—that had to come later.

CHAPTER EIGHT

Two months later

ZOE WAS STANDING by her desk, checking that all the documents she needed for that morning's important meeting in the city were loaded on her tablet. She was concentrating hard, but at the back of her mind she was aware of her senior accountant, Louise, chatting with someone at the external door to the office.

Her business—The Right Note: Accountancy and Tax—occupied the ground floor of a converted warehouse, part of a complex in Balmain. Zoe's living space was on the mezzanine level above.

She hoped the person at the door wasn't a client, hoping for an unscheduled appointment. That was the trouble with a client base drawn from musicians, writers, artists and entertainers—their idea of time didn't always match hers.

A glance at her watch told her she had time to catch the 9:15 a.m. ferry for the twenty-minute ride from Balmain into the city—but not a lot to spare.

She'd come to a crossroads with her business, and today's meeting with a potential buyer might help her decide which path to take. She needed to be at her most alert for the appointment—not flustered from being late. Louise would have to deal with the client.

Then Louise was by her side, her face flushed with excitement. 'Zoe, you've got no idea who's at the door, wanting to see you. *Mitch Bailey.*'

Zoe was too taken aback to do anything but stare at Louise.

'You know—the soccer player—the really hot one,' Louise added, her intonation implying that any red-blooded woman who didn't know who Mitch Bailey was needed her head read.

Zoe felt the blood drain from her face. Her heart started to hammer and a wave of nausea threatened to overwhelm her. Her hand went suddenly nerveless and her tablet started to slip from her grasp.

Louise caught the tablet and placed it on Zoe's desk. 'That's how I'd react if Mitch Bailey came to see me,' she said in a low, excited tone. 'He's even better-looking in person. Those eyes really are the most amazing green. And his smile… *Wow!*' Louise paused when she didn't get any reaction. 'Are you okay, Zoe?'

Zoe nodded. Cleared her throat. 'Of course I'm okay,' she choked out, in a reasonable facsimile of her normal speaking voice.

Mitch was here?

Louise nattered on. 'Do you think he's come to see us as a client? Someone might have recommended us to him. He wouldn't say. Just wants to see you. He's in the waiting area.'

Zoe cleared her throat. 'I…I'll see him.' She dragged in some deep, steadying breaths.

Mitch.

What was he doing in Sydney? What was he doing *here*?

As far as she knew Mitch was in Madrid, but her information wasn't up to date. On her return from Bali she'd found it impossible to stop thinking about him. Reliving over and over again the magical hours they'd shared at the villa. Every day she'd scoured the press for mentions of him, checked his official social media pages.

Ultimately she'd found it too distracting, too painful.

One night—that was all it was ever going to be. Mitch had made it very clear that there would be nothing more than that between them. An interlude with no future.

After a week she'd made a conscious decision—for her sanity's sake—not to check up on him, never to read the sports pages of the newspapers or watch the sports reports on television.

For all that, she hadn't been able to stop the dreams of him, of them together, that came to haunt her sleep. But she had nearly succeeded in putting him behind her—their time in Bali had been relegated to a bittersweet memory. And now he was here. It hardly seemed real.

Her hand went automatically to smooth her hair, and she pressed her lips together to ensure her lipstick was smooth.

'Don't worry about that. You look great,' whispered Louise, her eyes alight with curiosity.

Zoe hadn't confided in Louise or any other friend what had happened between her and Mitch in Bali.

'I wasn't worrying—' Zoe started to say, then stopped. Of *course* she was worrying about how she looked. *Mitch was here.*

Zoe wanted to sprint into the waiting area but forced herself to a sedate pace. She shouldn't read anything into this. Not after two months. Maybe Mitch was seeking some help with a double tax agreement with Spain. Or some other accountant-type advice.

She pasted a professional smile to her face. But her smile froze in stupefied admiration when she saw him. Mitch. Wearing a stylish tailored charcoal suit that emphasised his broad shoulders and strong, graceful body. He looked as if he'd stepped down off one of his billboards. The sexiest man alive was here in the waiting area of her company. And after the night they'd spent together she knew only too well how much he deserved that label.

Warm colour rushed into her cheeks when she realised it was the first time she'd seen him with clothes on—or more clothes than a pair of checked swim shorts.

Mitch seemed to freeze too, and she was conscious of him taking in every detail of her appearance. Thank heaven she'd taken extra trouble to look her best for the meeting. She was wearing a fitted deep pink designer suit—on sale at a bargain basement price but still designer—with slick black accessories. And she'd been up at the crack of dawn to make sure her hair and make-up were perfect.

She thought she'd got close to the image she wanted to portray to the management of the bigger firm—professional, but with a creative edge. To Mitch she hoped she appeared self-assured and independent. The kind of woman who took it completely in her stride when she was suddenly confronted by a man she had made love with two months ago. Without any communication whatsoever in between times. A woman who never cried into her pillow when she woke from her dreams of him.

She started to speak but had to clear her throat in order for the words to come out. In truth, she wasn't sure what to say. The last words she'd spoken to Mitch had been interspersed with sighs and murmurs of pleasure as they'd made love.

'Mitch—this is a surprise,' was all she could manage.

'Zoe.'

He took a few steps towards her and halted. She realised with a start that he seemed uncertain of his reception from her.

Her first impulse was to fling herself into his arms—that was where she wanted to be more than anything. But she wasn't a person who generally acted on impulse—unless an earthquake prompted her to do so, that was.

Instead she greeted him with a polite kiss on the cheek.

He held her briefly to him. Even that close contact was enough to send her senses skittering into hyper-awareness. Of his scent. His hard strength. The warmth of his body.

As he released her she stepped back and almost tripped on her stiletto heels. So much for seeming nonchalant, as if his presence didn't bother her at all.

'I was in Sydney and decided to look you up,' he said.

'How did you—?'

'Know where to find you? It didn't take advanced detective work to find an accountancy firm in a converted warehouse at Balmain.'

'Clever you,' she said, glad beyond measure that he had taken the trouble to track her down, uncertain as to his reason for doing so. 'But *why* are you in Sydney? Is it your knee?'

Mitch shook his head. 'My father had an accident.'

Zoe's hand flew to her mouth. 'I'm so sorry. Is he—?'

'He's fine. But I had to fly out to make sure for myself. I got here yesterday.'

He'd been in Sydney a day and she'd felt no awareness of him, had no 'Spidey-sense' knowledge that he was nearby. But then why should she? He was a one-time friend who'd become a one-time lover. That was all.

She was aching to ask him why he had come to see her, but instead took refuge in polite conversation.

'What happened to your dad?'

'He took up cycling—became a MAMIL.'

'You mean a Middle-Aged Man in Lycra?'

'That's the one. He went head over heels over his handlebars. Thankfully not in the path of any traffic. But he dislocated his collarbone, broke an arm and cracked a few ribs.'

'Ouch.' She shuddered in sympathy for the man she'd never met. 'Poor guy. Is he in hospital?'

'He's back home now. Complaining about having to stay in bed and making my mother's life hell.'

'But she must be so glad he's okay?'

His eyes crinkled in fond amusement. 'Of course she is.'

'Do your parents still live in Wahroonga?'

He nodded. 'In the same house I grew up in.'

The Bailey house was just a few streets away from her grandmother's house, where she'd spent such a miserable time. Since her return from Bali, Zoe had checked up on her grandmother. She was still alive, also still living in Wahroonga. But Zoe felt no desire to get in touch. Her life there seemed such a long time ago. The only good thing about that time had been Mitch.

'How long are you in Sydney for?' she asked, and immediately wished she could drag back the words. She didn't want him to think she was fishing for a chance to see him. But then again, he'd sought her out...

'I fly out tomorrow.'

'A short visit?' Her carefully modulated words masked her disappointment.

'Enough time to take you out to dinner.'

She swallowed hard. 'You mean tonight?'

'Are you free?'

Her pride didn't want him to think she was immediately available for a last-minute date. But she didn't want to play games. Especially not when the prize was an evening with Mitch. She couldn't lie to herself. Pride lost the battle.

'Of course I'm free,' she said.

Back in Madrid, Mitch hadn't been able to get Zoe out of his head. Her laughter, her passion, her vivacious face and gorgeous body had kept invading his thoughts.

He'd thrown himself into training. But still he'd thought of her. He'd dated other women. But each date had been hours wasted as in his mind he compared the poor woman—no matter how beautiful and charming—unfavourably with Zoe.

It had irked him. He didn't *want* to be distracted by thoughts of her. He didn't know why she'd slipped so thoroughly under his skin. Was it because *she'd* left *him* that morning two months ago? Left him and not made any effort to get in touch?

Yes, they'd agreed not to contact each other. But women had a tendency not to believe him when he told them he couldn't get involved. He'd had a few holiday flings before. With beautiful women who had recognised him and wanted to take whatever Mitch Bailey had to offer. He had always been the one to leave them to wake alone in their hotel room. And, when they'd tried to get in touch, to politely make it obvious that they were wasting their time.

Not Zoe. She'd left a note for the maid, but not for him. Was it a sense of unfinished business that bothered him? That made him unable to forget her?

He'd had no intention of seeing her when he'd unexpectedly come to Sydney. But he'd found himself looking her up—just out of interest, he'd told himself.

This morning he'd been on his way to a meeting with his Australian agent in the eastern suburbs. Somehow he'd detoured west to Balmain and down the narrow streets to this complex of converted warehouses. Now he'd asked Zoe out to dinner.

It was insanity. He should not be nudging open a door that should be kept firmly shut. Nothing had changed since Bali. There was still no room for Zoe or any other woman in his meticulously planned life. Yet here he was. And regretting it already.

Because the polished businesswoman standing before him wasn't the Zoe he remembered from their time together in Bali. That uninhibited Zoe had had tousled hair, worn no make-up, and had looked quite at home in nothing but a plain white towel—or nothing at all.

This Zoe—Corporate Zoe—was strikingly attractive in a very different way. The tailored, form-fitting suit and high heels, the shorter hair cut in an artfully layered style, the perfect make-up—all screamed candidate for Businesswoman of the Year. Not the girl who'd given as good as she'd got in a no-holds-barred water fight. Or in a big bed among tangled sheets under the slow flick of a ceiling fan on a steamy tropical night.

'Dinner tonight it is,' he said.

Though now he'd seen her he wondered if it was such a good idea.

In Madrid, he'd kept thinking about the connection they'd shared. A connection that had gone way beyond the physical and was like none he'd ever felt with a woman. But had it just been a holiday fling spiced by peril, the urgency of danger? Would they now struggle to find common ground?

'I'll look forward to it,' she said in her characteristic husky voice.

In any other woman he would find that voice an affectation. But Zoe's voice had had the same deep timbre at seventeen. Then it had seemed at odds with her schoolgirl persona. Now she'd grown into it—a sensual adult voice that sent awareness of her as a woman throbbing through him.

'Have you got anywhere in mind?'

He didn't. It had been a spur-of-the-moment decision to track her down. It would make him late for his meeting with his agent. Not that the agent would care. He made enough from his cut of Mitch's local earnings to put up with tardiness from his star client. Still, Mitch had called ahead to alert him. He believed in professional behaviour at all times.

He hadn't got as far as thinking about a restaurant. To see Zoe again, to see if she was still the woman who'd haunted his thoughts for two months, was all he had thought about.

'I'm going to be flat out all day so I'll look forward to dinner,' she said. 'I have a really important meeting with a company that—' She squealed. 'The ferry! I'm going to miss it! Be late for the meeting!'

Her face was screwed up in panic. Suddenly

she looked more approachable. More like the Zoe he knew—or thought he knew.

'Let me drive you,' he said. 'To the city?'

'No. I mean yes. The meeting *is* in the city. But peak-hour morning traffic will be too heavy; I'll still be late. A ride to the ferry stop would be helpful, though.'

'Can do,' he said. 'I'm parked in your car park.'

'How did you get past the security guard?'

He grinned.

Her lips lifted in a half smile. 'Of course. You're Mitch Bailey. Why did I bother to ask?'

She turned rapidly on her high heels, dashed out of the room, and returned seconds later with a stylish leather satchel flung over her shoulder.

'Let's go,' she said.

Walking more briskly than he'd imagine anyone else could in those heels, she took off across the wooden dock at the harbourside front of the building, past the small marina and around to the car park.

He pressed his key fob and lights flashed as the doors unlocked on the innocuous mid-range sedan he'd rented for the few days he was in

Sydney. It wasn't the type of car people would expect Mitch Bailey to drive, which was exactly why he'd chosen it. Choose a top-of-the-range European sports car like the one he had back in Madrid and he'd be inviting attention he didn't want.

So far he had evaded anyone outside his family and close circle of friends knowing he was back in Sydney. And Zoe too, of course. Where did she fit in? Friend? Lover? He found it impossible to categorise her.

She broke into a half run to get to the car and flung herself into the front passenger's seat after he'd opened the door for her. The car was suddenly filled with her energy, with her warm, heady scent—immediately familiar.

As he steered the car out of the car park she apologised for the rush. 'One of the bigger accounting firms has approached me to buy my business. My meeting this morning is with them.'

'That sounds impressive.' It didn't surprise him at all to hear she was doing well in the corporate world.

'It's flattering—that's for sure. They think I've tapped into a niche market they want a part of.'

'You don't sound one hundred per cent enthusiastic.' Since when had he been able to read her voice?

'I am and I'm not. They propose that my company would be absorbed by them as a specialised division, with me as the manager. But I worry that the vital personal touch might get lost if I lose control. My clients are an eccentric bunch and they could get scared off—even see my move as a betrayal. But I could help more people, expand the business to other states where there's a need for it.'

'It's a big decision.' He liked the way she was considering her clients—not just the potential gain for herself.

'There's pros and there's cons. I'll go in there this morning with an open mind.'

'You can tell me all about it tonight. I'll be interested to see what happens.'

As they spoke Mitch drove as fast as he could around the steep, narrow streets of Balmain, one of the oldest inner western suburbs of Sydney.

The streets were lined with quaint restored nine-teenth-century terrace houses and historic shop fronts. The area suited Zoe.

He turned into Darling Street and headed down towards the water. Ahead was the ferry terminal, framed by a view of the Sydney Harbour Bridge on the other side of the harbour.

'Thank heaven,' Zoe breathed when they saw the ferry was still docking. 'I wouldn't have made it without you.'

'You wouldn't have been late if I hadn't distracted you.'

'I'm glad you distracted me,' she said, tucking her satchel over her shoulder.

Mitch didn't know whether to read that as flirtatious or as a mere statement of fact. She was giving nothing away. Was she happy to see him or not? Had Bali meant anything to her?

She started to open the door before the car was completely stopped, then scrambled out. 'Gotta dash.'

She paused, half out and half in the car, revealing a stretch of slender leg that Mitch could not help but appreciate.

'I live on the floor above the office. Pick me up at seven-thirty tonight.'

'Right,' he said.

He reached out and put a hand on her arm. She stilled, and for a moment he thought she might shake his hand away from her.

'Good luck with the meeting,' he said. Had she thought he was going to say something else?

'I might need it,' she said, moving away. 'Thanks for the ride. See you tonight.'

She headed down to the ferry, which was now loading people across the gangplank. Commuting by ferry was an attractive part of Sydney living, he'd always thought.

The sight of her shapely back view in the bright pink suit as she broke into a half run down to the ferry was very appealing. She might be a different Zoe from the one he remembered from their time together in Bali, but she was just as hot in that subtly sexy way he'd found impossible to forget.

Which Zoe would he see tonight?

CHAPTER NINE

MITCH SAT ACROSS from Zoe at the harbourside restaurant he had booked for their dinner. He was not usually a man who found himself tongue-tied in conversation with a female companion. But tonight he was scraping around for something to say.

He and Zoe had already exclaimed over the spectacular view—the restaurant was situated on the north side of the harbour, right near the north pylon of the Sydney Harbour Bridge—and together they had marvelled at the sight of the lit-up ferries and pleasure boats criss-crossing the darkened waters of the harbour. They'd commented on the swimmers braving the winter to do laps below them, in the black-marked lanes of the Art Deco-style North Sydney Olympic Pool. And they'd each said how fond they were of the big grinning face that marked the entrance to Luna Park, the harbour-front amusement park next door.

Trouble was, that elephant was back. It was sitting below them, in the pale blue waters of that big swimming pool, looking up at them, taunting them. He and Zoe had spent the night together two months before, had shared the fear of possibly losing their lives, and yet neither of them had mentioned it. They were just acting as though they were old acquaintances catching up, skimming the surface with dinner table talk.

This morning he'd seen Corporate Zoe. Tonight he was with Sophisticated Zoe, stylish in a simple purple lace dress that covered her arms and chest but revealed glimpses of her creamy skin, the enticing curves of her breasts through the gaps in the lace. Her hair was slicked back smoothly to her head and she wore long drop earrings that moved when she turned. She was striking, elegant, self-assured.

Heads had turned when they'd walked in to the restaurant together—and they hadn't been looking at him. But he wanted the Zoe who'd turned *his* head wearing nothing but a skimpy white towel.

He remembered the flower he had tucked behind her ear that night in Bali—a prelude to the intimacy that had followed. Next morning he had found it, crumpled on her pillow. Never would he admit to anyone how he had scooped it up, wrapped it in a tissue from the bathroom and taken it back to Madrid with him.

He picked up the menu. 'Perhaps we should order?'

'Good idea,' she said.

'The menu looks good. Are you hungry?'

How inane was this conversation? He was flying back to Madrid the next day. The way this was going it didn't seem likely he would get a chance to talk to Zoe about anything important—let alone anything intimate.

He resisted the temptation to glance at his watch.

'Not excessively,' she said. 'I don't know that I've ever got over the Bali belly.'

At last—a reference to their recent shared past. He hoped the elephant was appeased.

'You're still feeling unwell?'

'Off and on.'

He frowned. 'That's a worry. You should get it checked out. You might have caught a tropical bug. They can have long-lasting consequences.'

He thought about telling her the story of his teammate who'd picked up a parasite through his bare feet in some country or other, but decided that was hardly dinner date conversation.

Zoe sighed. 'I know. I should go to the doctor. It's just I've been run off my feet at work—it's our busiest time of the year. All I do is work, work and more work.'

And date? Had she been going out with other guys? Had she found dating as unsatisfactory as he had?

The thought of her with another guy had tortured him back in Madrid. Had the ex-boyfriend come sniffing around? If he, Mitch, had had Zoe in his life he wouldn't have let her go easily.

Mitch gripped the side of the menu. *He had let her go.* He had made love to her all night and then just let her go.

Had he seriously expected he could just fly into

Sydney, show up on her doorstep and everything would be as it had been in Bali? He gritted his teeth. She wouldn't be independent, feisty Zoe if she just fell back into his arms. This was up to him. Unfinished business or not.

'Promise me you'll get to the doctor as soon as possible?' he said.

She smiled. 'I promise. Thank you for your concern.'

Their eyes met across the table. To his relief, he saw genuine appreciation in hers. That was at least a step up from guarded politeness.

'Good health is important,' he said. 'As I know only too well.'

'Your knee,' she said. 'I keep meaning to ask about it. Is it holding up?'

'So far, so good. I'm back to match fitness. Let's hope it stays that way. I've still got a lot to prove.'

'And your father?' She laughed, and her laughter had a nervous edge to it. 'No different from this morning, I guess. Sorry. Dumb question.'

'It wasn't a dumb question. He gets grumpier by the hour. Hates being inactive.'

'Did you get your interest in soccer from your dad?'

This wasn't how he'd pictured his reunion with sexy, passionate Zoe. Talking about his father. But if that was the way it was going he might as well throw his grandfather in too.

'Dad liked to kick a ball around. But it was my grandfather who really got me into soccer.' He smiled. 'Grandpa is English, and he would hate to hear me refer to football as "soccer".'

Zoe tilted her head attentively and her earrings swung. He wanted to reach over and still them. But would his touch be welcome? Her 'hands off' shield was very much in place.

Mitch realised that this evening might not go as he'd anticipated. After their meal was served he might get a polite brush-off and a cool kiss on the cheek like the one she'd given him this morning. He wasn't used to that. It stymied him.

'I didn't know your family was English?' she said.

'My father was born in England and grew up

there. In his twenties he came out to Australia on a gap year—only they didn't call it that in those days—met my mother here and stayed. We lived in north London, near my grandparents, for a year when I was eight. My grandfather got me hooked on soccer then. He used to take me to games…got me on a local team. He played for a London team himself when he was young. He lives and breathes the game.'

'He must be so proud of you now.'

'Not proud of me playing for a Spanish team. In fact he's disgusted.'

'Why don't you play for an English team?'

'I did. But a Spanish team bought me.'

'*Bought* you? Like a commodity?'

'I guess you could put it that way.'

'I know so little about the game.' She smiled. 'If an old schoolfriend hadn't become a soccer superstar I'd know even less.'

'Just ask if there's anything you'd like to know,' he said.

An old schoolfriend? He wanted to be so much more than that to her. Passionate, playful and sensual—that was the Zoe he remembered from

Bali. He couldn't settle for just friendship after she'd been all that to him. But then he couldn't offer her a relationship either.

In that regard nothing had changed since they'd last met in Bali. He could *not* let himself be distracted from his game by Zoe or any other woman. *He just couldn't.*

Last year he'd been briefly involved with a woman who had been too temperamental for his taste. When he'd broken it off with her there had been scenes, threats, confrontations—until he'd been forced to take out a restraining order against her.

It had been during that time when he had suffered his knee injury. Had the stress caused him to miss that split-second warning that two opposing players were headed towards him, clearly with the intent to take him out? He believed there was a good chance it had. It wouldn't happen again.

'Why do they call it "The Beautiful Game"? It sounds so...so *romantic*,' Zoe said.

His grandfather had often used the term, and had explained it to him many times as a kid. 'It's because the game is beautiful in its simplicity. It's not loaded with complex rules. If you have a ball you can play anywhere. Kids in their back yards or on dusty streets all over the world... highly paid players on a perfectly groomed pitch. It's an intelligent game—an individual's game as well as a team game. They say the first person to officially call it "The Beautiful Game" was the great Brazilian footballer Pelé.'

Mitch paused, conscious that he sounded as if he was preaching.

'I don't want to bore you...'

'You're not boring me at all. I can see how much you love your game. I admire your passion. No wonder it comes first with you.'

There was a hint of the Bali Zoe's teasing in her smile.

'Even if you *are* bought and sold like a racehorse.'

Zoe obviously had no idea of the money that changed hands at the top level of soccer. It wasn't the huge deal in Australia that it was in Europe, where players' incomes were splashed all over the press. Even he'd been astounded at the amounts that had poured into his bank account since he'd made it to the top. And that didn't include the sponsorship and endorsements his agent was always negotiating.

He was glad Zoe didn't seem to have any interest in his income. Lara had been only too aware of every possible euro, pound and dollar that might come his way. It had been a bitter realisation that Lara had been more in love with the money and the spotlight than she had been with him.

Ultimately she'd pressed for marriage—to secure that income, he'd believed. That had resulted in their final split—and a pay-out from him to stop her selling the story of their relationship to the media. To be fair to Lara, she'd stuck to the deal. It hadn't come as a shock when she'd taken up with another player not long afterwards.

Since then he'd steered clear of women he suspected of being interested not in the real Mitch Bailey but in his image and wealth. There were plenty of them around. Star footballers could be a target for the unscrupulous.

The waiter came alongside their table and

asked if he could take their order. Mitch quickly chose white fish and steamed vegetables in a lemon yogurt sauce. Zoe ordered a cheese and spinach vegetarian dish, explaining that she had lost her taste for meat since she hadn't been feeling well.

The conversation dwindled to virtually nothing. The elephant in the pool below was wallowing in the shallow end and spraying water through its trunk all over the swimmers. But neither he nor Zoe seemed able to call it to heel.

Zoe pleated the edge of her linen napkin, drew her finger around the edge of her water glass, played with her dangly earrings. She must be feeling as uncomfortable as he was. This was untenable.

Mitch reached across the table and stilled her hand with his. He looked into her eyes for a long, still moment.

'Zoe, I wish I could see what was in your thought bubbles,' he said. 'Because we're not making any headway talking and I don't have much time.'

* * *

Zoe gripped his hand in deep, heartfelt relief that Mitch had found the courage to say what she had been too knotted with nerves to say. He'd been so formal, his conversation so stilted—unless he was talking about soccer—that she'd feared the connection they'd shared in Bali had been completely severed. That she'd never see again the Mitch she'd shared both danger and ultimately pleasure with in the seclusion of her villa back in Seminyak.

'My thought bubbles?' she said, knowing her voice sounded shaky but unable to do anything about it except follow her words with a nervous laugh. 'Please don't ask me to sing them, because there's a guy over there with a cell phone who seems a tad too interested in us.'

In fact it looked as if the onlooker was about to snap a photo of them. Zoe withdrew her hand from Mitch's, kept her hands firmly on her lap.

'No need to sing,' Mitch said, with the disarming smile that struck straight to her heart.

He looked so impossibly handsome in that dark suit. She could still hardly believe he was here with her in Sydney. Her pulse quickened at the thought of what the evening might bring.

She took a deep, steadying breath. 'Okay. My thought bubbles say: "Apprehensive". "Awkward". "Curious".'

'"Curious"?' he said, his head tilted to one side, his eyes narrowed.

'Curious as to why you looked me up when you'd made it so clear you didn't want anything ongoing between us.'

'Fair enough,' he said. 'What about "awkward"?'

Under cover of the tablecloth overhang Zoe wrung her hands together. 'I'm anxious that I'll say the wrong thing—I'm second-guessing every word. I'm over the moon that you're here, but I don't want to appear too glad to see you in case…in case you think I'm wanting more from you. You made your agenda for the future very clear.'

'Which explains "Apprehensive"…' said Mitch.

She nodded, unable to speak through a sudden lump of emotion. She blinked against unwelcome, mortifying tears. 'Yes,' she forced herself to say.

'My thought bubbles are pretty much the same,' he said slowly. 'I'm worried that we seem like strangers to each other.'

'Exactly,' she said. 'And I don't know what to do about it.'

Mitch leaned across the table. 'I thought about you a lot when I was back in Madrid, Zoe.'

'I…I thought about you too.' She didn't want to give too much away. Such as the fact she still awoke from dreams of him to find herself in tears.

'We didn't get to say goodbye in Bali.'

There was accusation in his voice and affronted pride in his eyes.

Zoe realised that Mitch, the celebrity sportsman, was not used to being left by a woman. Not in those circumstances. She hadn't meant to take the upper hand by creeping out of the villa without awakening him to say goodbye. It had saved her an awkward moment. Mitch might be used to such no-strings encounters. She was not.

'It seemed better that way,' she said, finding

it difficult to meet his eyes. 'We'd agreed it...it would only be for that night.'

'When I woke up and you weren't there I was gutted.'

'It...it was difficult to leave you, but it would have been worse to face you. I...I had never been in that situation before. I didn't know how to deal with it.'

She'd sobbed in the taxi all the way to the airport. Then huddled into her seat on the plane for the entire six-hour flight home to Sydney, desperately trying not to sob some more.

His mouth twisted wryly. 'Severing all contact between us seemed the right thing at the time. When I got back to Madrid and had time to think, it seemed all kinds of wrong. I wanted to get in touch. But I thought that wouldn't be fair on you. My situation hadn't changed.'

'I wanted to contact you too. But I...I didn't want to seem like a...like a groupie. I...know you're probably plagued by them.'

Mitch's so-expressive eyebrows rose. 'Don't ever think that. You are nothing like that. Not that I've had anything to do with groupies, and nor am I criticising them, but I see what goes on.'

'Each to his own,' she murmured, glad that Mitch had distanced himself from that aspect of his fame. But still... She couldn't believe their one night in Seminyak had been the first no-strings incident for *him*. He was idolised by women.

'You're smart, gorgeous, funny. I couldn't stop thinking about you.'

On the surface, those words should have sounded romantic. But Zoe detected an under-tone of annoyance—even anger. It was as if she were some unwelcome prickly thorn, pressing into his consciousness. She wasn't at all sure she liked it.

She swallowed hard. 'I...I couldn't stop think-ing about you either,' she said. 'I tried, though. I really tried. Otherwise I would have gone crazy. I purposely avoided the sports pages, the interna-tional sports news. That's why I got such a shock to see you this morning. I had no idea you were in Australia.'

'I was going crazy in my own way, trying to

find out what *you* were doing. You've got such rigid privacy settings on your social media.'

'You tried to stalk me on social media?' Zoe tried to suppress her laughter so it didn't attract attention. 'Imagine...Mitch Bailey stalking me— I'm flattered.'

'I wouldn't say "stalking" you,' he said, with what she took to be more affronted pride. 'More... attempting research into your comings and goings. And failing dismally—courtesy of your firewalls.'

'I told you...I'm a private person.' She looked sideways at the guy on the other table with the camera phone. His attention was now on his meal, not on Mitch, thank heaven.

'Did you date other guys?'

The directness of Mitch's question stunned her. But she didn't have to search for an answer. 'No. I didn't want to.'

How could any other man have compared to Mitch? Trouble was, no other guy she'd met in the meantime had attracted her. That night in Bali had shown her what it could be like between a man and a woman. Not just the lovemaking.

It had also been about the shared laughter, the joy, the connection that to her had been so much more than physical.

She wanted Mitch but he could not offer her what she needed—commitment, love. One day she'd meet someone who could offer her more than one night in his busy schedule. She had no intention of putting her life on hold for Mitch Bailey.

No matter that just sitting opposite him at a restaurant table was thrilling her in a way being with any other man never had. No. She hadn't even looked at another man in the last two months.

His relief was palpable. 'Good,' he said.

Zoe gasped. His reaction was a bit rich. What did he mean, *'good'*?

He had no rights over her personal life. They'd made no commitment—hadn't even exchanged contact details. She was free to date whom she darn well pleased. The fact that she hadn't met anyone who came anywhere near him was beside the point.

She wanted to say something but bit her tongue. It was an unexpected bonus to see Mitch again.

She didn't want to ruin it by being combative. What was the point?

'What about you?' she said.

He shrugged. 'I went out with a few women.'

Jealousy—fierce and unexpected—stabbed her so hard she flinched. She couldn't bear to think of him with someone else. And that was crazy, considering the nature of their relationship. Not that you could even call it a relationship. Heck, you couldn't even call it a *friendship*. She couldn't find a label to paste on whatever it was with her and Mitch Bailey.

She didn't say anything, just raised an eyebrow. While she churned inside with jealousy.

'It was a disaster,' he said. 'I kept comparing them to you and they fell short. I gave up on dating.'

What was she meant to infer from that? 'Oh...' was all she managed to choke out, with her jealousy somewhat appeased.

For a long moment their eyes met. But if she was searching for more she didn't find it. His gaze was guarded.

'It's good to see you, Zoe.'

'It's good to you, too,' she said.

'There's something there…more than friendship,' he said.

A secret thrill that he had acknowledged it pulsed through her. 'So what are we going to do about it?' she asked eventually. 'Fact is, I still live in Sydney and you still live in Madrid.'

'And that isn't going to change,' he said. 'For all the reasons I explained to you before. But we could keep in touch on the internet.'

'You mean I'd have to let down my firewalls for you?' she said, in a feeble attempt at humour.

'Yes. You'd have to let me scale those walls.'

Did she detect a note of triumph in his voice? Mitch liked to win. *For what purpose?*

She found herself pleating her napkin again. 'Will you be back in Australia any time soon?'

It would be torture to wait months and months to see him.

'It's not likely,' he said. 'Not until next year, when the season ends. Playing league football is more than a full-time commitment.'

'That…that's a long time.' How could they possibly maintain anything resembling more than a casual friendship on that time scale?

'Are you planning a trip to Europe any time soon?' he asked.

She shook her head. 'I'm not sure…'

She'd blown her vacation budget with the Bali trip. There was no spare cash for an expensive trip to Europe, and she didn't believe in paying for vacations on credit.

'That's a shame. You could have visited me in Madrid,' he said. 'I have a very nice apartment in old Madrid. You'd like it.'

'I…I'm sure I would,' she said. 'I'd like to see Spain some day. That would give me an incentive to study Spanish again.'

Would it be worth a credit card binge to see Mitch in Madrid? Excitement started to bubble up at the prospect.

'Let's think about how we can make it work,' he said. 'I have a full schedule of training, then pre-season matches in England, France and Italy before the season starts the last week in August. We could fit in a visit when I'm playing at home? That is if it coincided with your trip?'

Zoe was about to engage seriously with Mitch about what might be a good time for her to visit Madrid if she happened to be travelling to Europe—and then it hit her.

Mitch wasn't actually *inviting* her to visit him. He wasn't putting himself out in any way. Such a trip would be all about her running around the world to meet him at his convenience. For *what*? A bootie call? If she just happened to be in the neighbourhood? He was hedging his bets in a major way.

She swallowed down hard against a sudden bitter taste in her mouth. There would be no trip to Madrid for her to chase after Mitch in the hope of spending time with him. In her book, old-fashioned as it might be, the man did the chasing.

Before she could explain this to Mitch the waiter arrived at their table with their food and proceeded to describe in detail the meals they'd ordered. She put down her napkin—by now pleated to a narrow strip—and thanked the waiter.

She looked at the food on her plate—beautifully cooked and presented. But she didn't feel like eating. As the aroma of the food filled her nostrils a wave of nausea overtook her. Mitch was right. She needed to check out this recurring illness. Or was it disappointment that was making her feel like this?

Mitch picked up his fork. 'You haven't told me how your meeting went today with your potential purchaser?'

Zoe was grateful for the change of subject. She pushed her food around her plate with her fork. 'They made me a generous offer,' she said. 'Set out some attractive if constricting terms and conditions. We talked about expanding my specialised service into other states.'

'And...?'

Zoe shrugged. 'I'm still not convinced. I'm a very independent person—used to running my own show. I'm not sure how I'd take to being at the beck and call of a boss.'

'I believe that,' said Mitch. 'So, how did you leave it with them?' He seemed genuinely interested.

'I told him I'd consider it. In the meantime I talked with my friend Louise, who works with me. I've been thinking of bringing her into the company as a full partner. She'd have to *buy* in, of course. Then we could think of expanding. We already spend quite a bit of time commuting to Melbourne, to service the clients we have there.'

'You're very ambitious,' he said, and she appreciated the admiration in his voice.

'Yes,' she said. 'That's one reason I'm seriously considering the offer. Perhaps I can move higher in a bigger firm than I could on my own. It's all worth considering.'

'You've got a big decision to make. It will be interesting to see what you decide to do,' he said. 'Be sure you let me know.'

Was he just saying that? Did he really want to stay in touch?

'Yes…' she said non-committally.

'We've both come a long way since we were seventeen,' he said, his brows drawn thoughtfully together. 'Me where I am—you with your own business.'

Startled, she looked up. 'I guess we have.'

'We've both still got a long way to go,' he said. She knew his career was all-important to him, and he'd made it very clear that he'd put his personal life on hold. But she aspired to more than business success. Success for her also meant a fulfilling personal life one day. That lifetime love she aspired to—and a happy family life.

With a wrench to her heart that was almost physical she realised it would never happen with Mitch—no matter the strength of her feelings for him. By the time he reached a stage when he wanted to settle down she would be long in his past.

CHAPTER TEN

MITCH PREDICTED ALMOST to the minute the time when the guy with the camera phone Zoe had been keeping her eye on would make his way to their table: after he and Zoe had finished their main courses and the waiter had removed their plates.

Mitch knew from the guy's respectful attitude and the phone held so visibly in his hand that it wouldn't be a problem. But Zoe's eyes widened in alarm.

He remembered what she'd said about being a private person. Even a casual friendship with him opened her up to possible confrontations with the paparazzi.

'Mitch, I'm a huge fan—so is my son,' the guy with the camera said. 'Could I have a photo with you, please?'

'Of course,' said Mitch, looking around for the waiter.

'I'll take the photo,' said Zoe, jumping up from her seat.

Full marks to Zoe. That was one way of avoiding being in a photo. Maybe he didn't need to worry too much about her coping with any possible publicity.

She took the guy's phone and made a fuss of posing Mitch and his fan.

'Thank you,' the guy said to Zoe. 'Can I get one of me and you two together now?'

'I… I…' Zoe stuttered.

'Of course,' said Mitch.

'It's for my wife,' his fan explained. 'She didn't like Lara one little bit and will be happy to see you with such a lovely young lady.'

Again Mitch was struck by how public his life had become. It was highly improbable that this man's wife had ever actually met Lara. The woman just hadn't liked the Lara she'd seen in the media.

'Zoe is an old friend of mine,' said Mitch, 'and she is indeed lovely.'

Zoe was obviously too stupefied to object. Mitch called the waiter over to take the photo.

That would save both him and Zoe from any un-flattering 'selfie'.

After the fan had gone happily on his way Zoe turned to him. She shuddered. 'Do you have to put up with that all the time?'

'I'm never rude to a fan. He was a good guy. We made his evening—his wife and son will be chuffed.'

'I found it disconcerting, to say the least,' Zoe said, in a tone so low it was nearly a whisper. 'Especially what he said about Lara.'

She looked nervously around her, as if there might be a photographer at every table. Fact was: there could be. Everyone with a smartphone was a potential paparazzo these days. But that came with the turf. Mitch had learned to deal with it.

'C'mon—let's leave if it's making you uncomfortable,' he said. 'We can grab a coffee somewhere else, if you'd like.'

'There are a few nice cafés around here,' she said. 'We could walk along the boardwalk by the harbour.'

'Good idea. We can work that dinner off.'

Not that she'd eaten much.

She hesitated. 'I...I won't end up on some gossip website, will I? You know—"Mystery brunette on harbourside stroll with visiting soccer star"?'

Mitch thought about her helicopter fears back at the villa in Bali. She was right—they did exist on different planets. Zoe was so unlike Lara, who would have been preening at the thought of being in the spotlight.

'That guy? Highly unlikely,' he said. 'He'll show the photo around to the other parents at his boy's soccer club though, I'll bet.'

Although freedom from other, less scrupulous people, who cashed in on opportunistic amateur shots, he couldn't guarantee. But he'd seen no one suspicious tonight. No one would imagine he'd be in Sydney when he should be in Europe, playing 'friendly' matches to warm up for the season to come.

But he'd had to see if his father was okay. And then there was Zoe. He'd be kidding himself if he denied that he'd leaped at the opportunity to see Zoe.

Now he realised that if at the back of his mind

he'd hoped meeting with her again would leave him cold—would rid him of his attraction to her—then he'd been totally mistaken. She was even hotter than he'd remembered. There was nothing he wanted more than to take up where they'd left off in Bali.

Of course Zoe tried to pay her share for the dinner. He'd anticipated that, and had already settled the bill when Zoe came back to the table after going to the ladies' room.

'I insist on paying for the coffee, then,' she said, with that already familiar stubborn tilt to her chin.

Yes, Zoe was *very* different from the other women in his orbit.

They walked out of the restaurant into the narrow back street of Milson's Point. It was a typically mild Sydney winter night, but Zoe wrapped her arms around herself and shivered. She reached into her purse and pulled out a filmy scarf she wrapped around her shoulders.

'I can't imagine *that* will keep you warm,' he said.

'I'm fine,' she said, with an edge to her voice, not meeting his eyes.

'No, you're not, you're shivering,' he said. 'Come here.'

He pulled Zoe into his arms and held her very close, until her shivering stopped, and finally she relaxed against him with a small sigh, her head resting against his shoulder Mitch didn't know whether to interpret that sigh as relief or defeat.

He closed his eyes, the better to savour the sensation of having her close. He inhaled the sharp sweet scent of her—a Balinese blend of lemongrass and jasmine, she'd told him when he'd asked—that brought back heady memories of that brief, intense time they'd spent together in her villa.

This. This was what he'd longed for back in the echoing emptiness of his apartment in Madrid. He should not be letting himself feel this. But he heaved a huge sigh of relief that she made no effort to break away from him.

'Warm now?' he asked, his voice a husky rasp.

'Yes,' she murmured against his shoulder.

She pulled away, but remained within the circle of his arms, her own arms around his waist. She looked up to him. 'Thank you.'

Her face was in semi-shadow, her earrings glinting in the reflected light from the illumination of the giant grinning face of the entrance to Luna Park that loomed behind him. The sounds of carnival music and kids screaming on rides travelled on the still air.

'What next, Zoe?' he asked.

Her eyes told him that she knew he wasn't talking about the direction of their walk.

'Whatever we both want,' she said slowly.

She lifted her mouth to him. He didn't hesitate to accept the invitation. He bent his head and kissed her. But his kiss was brief and tender—he was as aware as Zoe of the possibility of interested eyes on them.

'I've been wanting to do this all day,' he said.

'Me too,' she said, a catch to her voice.

A taxi drew up and a noisy group of people got out, obviously heading for the restaurant. Zoe turned away from his embrace. As if by silent consent he took her arm and they headed away, to leave the restaurant behind them.

He walked beside her down the steep steps near the giant smile at the entrance to Luna Park to reach the harbour walk that ran by the harbour's edge, from Lavender Bay to Milson's Point. Despite the mildness of the night there was a hint of a breeze blowing off the water.

As they reached the boardwalk Zoe shivered again, and pulled the flimsy excuse for a wrap tighter to her. 'I don't know why I didn't wear a coat,' she said.

Mitch didn't hesitate to put his arm around her and pull her to his side. To hell with the possibility of cameras. He and Zoe weren't the only couple strolling along the boardwalk with their arms around each other. They would just blend in. He wanted her near him.

It had been such a long time since he'd lived in Sydney, and he found himself caught up in the magic of Sydney Harbour on a calm, clear night. He blocked the thought that being with Zoe was part of the magic. He could not allow himself to think that. Not when he was leaving tomorrow. Not when he didn't know when he would see her again.

In silence, they walked past the Art Deco façade of the pool and under the arch of the bridge.

He didn't know whether the silence was companionable or choked with words better left unsaid.

Once they reached the eastern side of the bridge he and Zoe paused and leaned on the cast-iron railing to look across the water to the Opera House, its giant white sails lit up with a beauty that was almost ethereal.

'Do you think you'll ever come back to live in Australia?' Zoe asked.

He shrugged. 'Maybe. I don't know. Sydney will always be home. But for the foreseeable future Europe is where I want to be.'

At the age of twenty-seven he saw that future stretch way ahead of him, exciting with possibilities. He was cautiously optimistic about his knee. Who knew how far he could go?

'Tell me again when you have to go back to Madrid? It really is tomorrow?'

'Yes,' he said.

The single word seemed to toll like a warning of impending doom.

Zoe was looking ahead at the view so he couldn't see her face. But he felt her flinch.

'So…so we only have tonight,' she said, again

with that little catch to her voice that wrenched at him.

'Yes,' he said. 'I fly out in the afternoon.'

A big harbour cruiser went by and a blast of brash music shattered the tranquillity of the scene. Did Zoe like that kind of music? Probably not. He realised how much he didn't know about her. How much he wanted to know. One day, perhaps...

'I wish it wasn't such a long way between Australia and Spain,' she said wistfully.

It remained unspoken between them that it wasn't only the twenty-two-hour flight that separated them. His need to prove himself over and over without distraction stood in their way. Mitch liked Zoe. *Really* liked her. But he couldn't let that liking and his attraction grow into anything deeper. This wasn't the time for him. No matter how he might find himself wishing it could be different.

'Me too,' he said. 'But even if we lived closer I still couldn't promise anything more than—'

'Friendship with benefits?' she said.

He followed her gaze as she looked down into

the dark green water of the harbour. Small waves from the cruiser's wash were smashing against the sandstone supports of the railing.

'Very occasional benefits,' she added, in a tone so low he scarcely caught it.

Put like that, it sounded so callous.

With his fingers, Mitch tilted her chin upwards so she had to meet his gaze. 'Zoe, I wish it could be more. Who knows what could happen in the—?'

'Future?' she said. She reached up to silence him with her finger on his mouth, as she had done before. 'Let's not talk about the future.'

The thinly veiled sadness in her eyes made his resolve waver. 'Who knows? One day…' he said.

Slowly she shook her head. 'It seems to me we can only take this one day at a time. So we'd better make the most of the hours we've got left.'

'Agreed,' he said.

He hoped her idea of a wonderful way to fill the hours coincided with his. Alone. Private. Clothes optional.

'How long since you've been to Luna Park?' she asked.

He paused, surprised at the question. 'Years and years,' he said.

'Me too,' she said. 'Not since I was at uni. The noise and music coming from there sounds fun. Let's walk through before we go and find a coffee shop.'

Mitch was too startled to reply. It was hardly *his* idea of making the most of the hours they had left together.

'Sounds like a plan,' he said, with an effort to sound enthusiastic.

'We can just walk around and look,' she said.

His parents had taken him and his brothers to Luna Park when he was very young. Then it had been closed for years, and he hadn't revisited it until he was a teenager. He'd taken his training so seriously that amusement parks hadn't been much on the agenda. Besides, Lara had looked down her nose at what she'd thought was a plebeian form of entertainment.

'That could be fun,' he said.

He took Zoe's hand in his as they walked along the harbour back towards the bright lights and clashing noises of Luna Park. She looked up at him and smiled, and he smiled back.

Holding hands with Zoe. Who would have thought something so simple, so everyday, would make him feel so...? He thought hard about what this feeling was. *Happy.* Being with Zoe made him feel happy.

As they walked under the big grinning face into the entertainment park he gave it a mental salute.

CHAPTER ELEVEN

ZOE HAD NO IDEA why she'd suggested going to Luna Park with Mitch. Panic, perhaps? Prolonging the inevitable? What she really wanted was to be alone with him, somewhere quiet and romantic.

But she was struggling with the 'friends with occasional benefits' scenario. She wanted Mitch with a deep, yearning hunger—a craving. It was impossible to stop sneaking glances at him to admire his profile, the shape of his mouth, the set of his shoulders. She found everything about him exciting. The thought of the sensual pleasures they had shared made her shiver with remembered ecstasy. But she balked at the idea of being his occasional lover.

Bali had been different. The circumstances had been extraordinary. She'd believed there would be only the one time. That she would be able to put their encounter behind her almost as if it had been a dream. It hadn't been easy to forget him. And now he was back in her life, but on very uncertain ground. It might be commonplace for a celebrity sports star to do the 'occasional lover' thing. Not so for an ordinary girl with dreams of a once-in-a-lifetime love. A girl teetering on the edge of falling in love with him.

Walking hand in hand with Mitch like any other couple strolling along the harbour walk on a mild Thursday evening felt so *right*. She loved the feel of his much larger hand enfolding hers, the way their shoulders nudged, the subtle intimacy. As if they were meant to be together.

But tomorrow he would be on his way to Madrid again. And she would be left with perhaps the comfort of an occasional phone call. She had no illusions. Once he was again immersed in his game she would not be at the front of his mind.

Luna Park was chaotic and fun. It was the perfect distraction from the hollow feeling of loss Zoe felt at the thought of Mitch flying back to Madrid the next day. Her spirits had lifted as soon as she was surrounded by the bright lights, music and carnival atmosphere.

Set right on the harbour, surrounded by some of the most expensive real estate in Australia, the old-fashioned fun fair operated in the evenings during school vacations despite the protests of its well-heeled neighbours. Zoe supported its right to be there—the Sydney icon had existed since 1935, built on land that had been the construction site for the building of the Sydney Harbour Bridge.

For many older Sydney-siders the place was loaded with nostalgia. Zoe's maternal grandmother had brought her here a few times by ferry when she was a little girl—it was one of her only memories of her as she had died when Zoe was seven.

She sometimes wondered how different her life would have been if *that* grandmother had been alive when her parents had died and she had been put into *her* care.

Once through the entrance, she and Mitch were surrounded by rides and sideshows on both sides.

She looked around and laughed. 'Just watching the rides is making me feel dizzy.'

'They're fast and furious, all right,' said Mitch. 'What do you want to ride first? The Wild Mouse rollercoaster?'

What had she got herself into? Zoe pretend to cower, but her fear was real. 'Uh…I'm actually terrified of it.'

Mitch couldn't mask his disappointment. He looked longingly upwards to where the brightly painted carriages rattled at great speed along the tracks. Excited squeals and shrieks rang out every time a carriage swung around.

'I didn't take you for such a wimp, Zoe,' he said, but the way his eyes crinkled and he squeezed her hand let her know he was teasing.

She looked up at him. 'I have a confession to make. When it comes to rides I *am* a wimp. When I'm on something like the Wild Mouse, screaming, it's not from excitement but from genuine fear.'

'You *have* to be kidding me?' he said, raising his expressive eyebrows. 'A fun fair is all about exhilaration and terror and regretting that last hot dog you ate. Why did you bring me here if you weren't prepared for the screaming? Does that mean we don't even get to go on the Hair Raiser?'

He waved his arm towards a ride where strapped-in riders were raised up high in the sky, only to be plummeted back to earth at a frightening pace, screaming all the way.

To Zoe's eyes it was terrifying. She pulled a repentant face. 'Sorry. You wouldn't get me up on that thing in a million years. It would be an amazing view of the city, up so high, but I'd have my eyes tightly shut and wouldn't see a thing. I'd forgotten how scary these rides are.'

'So we're only going on *girly* rides, are we? Don't expect me to ride with you on that wussy carousel.' Mitch glowered, but ruined the effect with a smile that insisted on breaking through his frown.

'Actually, I rather like those pretty ponies. Sure you wouldn't join me on one? Safe and sedate— just how I like it.'

Safe and sedate? There was nothing safe or sedate about the way she felt about Mitch...

Mitch crossed his arms across his chest. 'No to the painted ponies. You will never, *ever* get me on one of those things.'

'I love the giant slides. Or I could challenge you on the dodgem cars?'

'Now you're talking,' he said.

They only had to wait a few minutes for the next dodgem session. Zoe liked the way Mitch wasn't the least bit self-conscious about lining up with a crowd of mainly teenagers. Looking around her, she saw she wasn't the only woman in a dressy dress and heels.

'Shall we share a car?' she asked as they got ready to run and claim one.

'I want one of my own,' he said.

Once Zoe was strapped into her bumper car and the music started she stepped on the accelerator too hard—and crashed her rubber bumpers straight into Mitch's car.

'Gotcha!' she called, smiling.

'A challenge?' he said, assuming a racing driver's position behind the wheel, his expression deadly serious. 'We're talking professional, here. I drive to win.'

'You're on,' she said. 'I drive to destroy.'

As they took to the circuit and thumped and bumped their electric cars into each other, and the surrounding cars, Zoe started to laugh. By the time the session came to an end she was paralysed by giggles.

Mitch helped her out of her car. 'That was so much fun,' she said as her giggles subsided.

'You were determined to thrash me,' he said.

'And I did,' she said.

'I would dispute that. I counted the bumps and I came out ahead.'

'Oh, really?' she challenged. 'How many bumps?'

'I was five more than you. Do you concede defeat?' he said, grinning.

'I wasn't counting, so I have to believe you,' she said, narrowing her eyes in mock anger.

'That said, I'll allow that you were a worthy opponent.'

'I just wish I'd thought to count the bumps— I'm sure I came out on top.'

'I enjoyed it,' he said. 'Kids' stuff, but fun.'

'The thing is,' she said, 'I don't think I ever acted that childish when I was a child.' She tucked her arm through his. 'C'mon—let's try another ride.'

They wandered through the fun fair until Zoe stopped at the Laughing Clowns sideshow.

'I was so scared of these things when I was little,' she said.

A row of motorised vintage clown heads with open mouths moved from side to side, ready for people to throw small balls in the hope of winning a prize.

'You seem so fearless, Zoe, and yet you have all these hidden fears,' Mitch said.

He rested his hand on the back of her neck and the casual contact sent shivers of awareness coursing through her.

'Not so hidden,' she said. 'Lots of people are frightened of clowns. There's even a name for it—coulrophobia. I still don't like them.'

He leaned in closer. 'What else are you frightened of, Zoe?' he asked in an undertone.

Of falling in love with you and getting my heart pulverised, she thought, but she would never put voice to that.

She forced her voice to sound unconcerned. 'Earthquakes, of course. But we've been there—

done that. Nothing much else—what about you?' she said. 'Snakes? Spiders? Sharks?'

He shook his head. 'I wouldn't go out of my way to encounter any of those, but I'm not scared of them.' He paused. 'I...I fear failure.'

She stared at him, too surprised at his admission to speak. 'But you're so successful,' she said eventually.

'You're only as good as your last game,' he said. 'Failure on the world stage isn't a pretty thing.'

'So if you don't come back fighting this season, with your knee fixed, you'll consider it failure?'

He stilled and went silent, and Zoe sensed his thoughts had turned inwards.

'Yes,' he said, after a long pause.

The single word was a full-stop to the thought and she knew there was nothing further to be said.

Mitch looked at the clowns, challenge in his stance. 'I'm not scared of *these* things. I'm going to beat 'em,' he said with confident arrogance. His eyes narrowed as he assessed the clowns' state of play before taking out his wallet.

The young guy behind the counter explained that Mitch needed to get five balls into the clowns' mouths—each clown varying in points scored. Mitch paid for and took the balls. Then he focussed his gaze, took aim and, one at a time, shot all five balls into the gaping mouths of the clowns.

Zoe clapped her hands together, doing a little dance of excitement. 'Well done!'

'Not bad,' said Mitch, with studied nonchalance.

It was nothing—absolutely nothing—compared to his achievements in soccer, but she was there with him and that made it special to her.

Would she ever be able to come to Luna Park again without him? There would be memories everywhere.

The sideshow attendant handed over a bright blue teddy bear as Mitch's prize. But Mitch pointed to a little white stuffed dog, wearing a miniature Aussie-style hat.

'That one, please,' he said. He turned to Zoe and handed it to her. 'For you,' he said. 'To remember what fun we've had this night.'

Zoe took the toy and clutched it to her, ridiculously pleased. Unwelcome tears stung her eyes. She swallowed against a sudden lump in her throat. 'Th...thank you. It's very cute.'

Did he have to remind her how fleeting their time together was?

Before Mitch had a chance to say anything more, a thirty-something man who had been standing behind them, waiting his turn for the clowns, turned to Mitch. 'That was awesome, mate.'

Mitch nodded in acknowledgement of the praise. 'Focus is what it takes,' he said.

Zoe could see recognition dawn in the man's eyes before a big grin split his face.

'As Mitch Bailey knows only too well!' he said. 'Mitch, you're meant to be in *Spain*.'

He reeled off an impressive list of European fixtures in which Mitch's team was scheduled to play. Then he pulled out a crumpled flyer for a restaurant.

'Can I get your autograph?'

Mitch obligingly autographed the piece of paper, then shook the man's hand. As the man walked away he looked back over his shoulder to

Mitch several times, grinning. Zoe didn't have to be able to read his thought bubbles to understand the man's delight in having met his idol.

The full weight of Mitch's responsibilities to his fans seemed to settle on her shoulders. She began to comprehend his determination that nothing could come between his return to top form. Not her. Not any woman. But she refused to let it suppress her spirits.

Tonight was hers.

Mitch looked down at Zoe. Her face was flushed, and strands of her dark hair had come loose from its severe style to waft around her face. Laughter still curved the corners of her mouth and her eyes shone.

He reached out and smoothed the errant hair back into place. He had never wanted her more.

'Thank you,' she murmured. 'I must look a mess.'

'You could never look a mess,' he said. 'You look like a woman who's faced a mighty dodgem battle and won through.'

She was breathtaking. Attractive, yes, but also

vibrant, smart and straightforward. Zoe Summers was unlike any other woman he'd met.

Something deep inside him seemed to turn over as he looked into her eyes. When they'd been battling with so much fun, intent on the dodgem car circuit, he'd been struck by how effortlessly they got on together. There were no games, no pretence. It had taken him back to their water fight in the pool in Bali—how much he'd enjoyed that too. And that was on top of how superlatively they'd got on in bed.

It struck him what it was that drew him so strongly to her—she grounded him. He knew she didn't give a toss about his money or fame. She'd been on his side when they were teenagers. He firmly believed she was on his side now. He could be himself with her, in a way he couldn't with anyone else outside his family.

Her idea to come to Luna Park had been inspired. She'd relaxed, and so had he. He could think of no other place he'd rather be right now than here with her.

Not even Madrid.

That was a dangerous thought.

He had to block it.

If he wasn't careful this woman could change his life. And he did *not* want to deviate from the path he had set himself.

All he had with Zoe was tonight. He'd better remember that.

'Time to go?' she asked.

'Yes,' he said. 'We can drive to a coffee shop.'

'Or have coffee at my house?' she said.

Coffee or something more? He just wanted to spend time with her, no matter how it might end up.

'Great idea,' he said.

'Let's go, then,' she said. 'Before more of your fans realise Mitch Bailey is in town.'

He took her hand and led her out of Luna Park, striding so fast she had to ask him to slow down, breathlessly reminding him that she was wearing high heels.

He slowed his pace on the steep stairs up to the narrow street where he'd parked the car. Then, in the shadows the streetlights did not illuminate, at last he kissed her—fiercely, possessively—and she kissed him back with equal fervour.

CHAPTER TWELVE

ZOE DIDN'T EVEN MENTION coffee when they got back to her place. Mitch didn't give her the chance to. He made sure she scarcely had time to draw breath between urgent, drugging kisses. He was too conscious of the hours, the minutes, the seconds ticking by until he had to say goodbye to her.

She didn't protest. Laughing, breathless, she took him—stumbling as they tried to walk and kiss at the same time—through the reception area, where he'd waited for her that morning, past an office and into a large living room. She fumbled with light switches, missing half of them with unsteady fingers, so they could see where they were going.

Between kisses he registered that the room was all industrial chic, with soaring ceilings, open beams, rough old brickwork and wide hardwood floors. Further through was another living area with sleek modern furniture. Open metal stairs led to a mezzanine that Mitch assumed was her bedroom. The east-facing wall comprised floor-to-ceiling industrial windows that framed a night-time view across Mort Bay to Goat Island.

But he was too busy feasting his eyes on Zoe to bother with the view, no matter how spectacular.

Still kissing, they landed on the white sofa, laughing as their limbs tangled and tripped them. A large slumbering tabby cat yowled its protest at their occupation of its sofa and shot off towards the kitchen.

Mitch found the zipper of Zoe's purple dress and tugged it down over the smooth skin of her shoulders. Her scent filled his nostrils: warm, womanly, arousing. Her curves, soft and lovely, moulded to his chest, her thighs pressed to his. *At last.* This was what he had been wanting for two long months. *Zoe.* There had been no other woman in between.

He shrugged off his jacket as she divested him of his tie and fumbled with fingers that weren't steady at the small buttons on his shirt.

A pulse throbbed at the base of her neck and he

bent his head to press a kiss there. She clutched at his shoulders with a murmur of pleasure deep in her throat that sent his senses into overdrive. He broke the kiss. Pulled back. Her eyes were unfocused with passion, her mouth swollen from his kisses.

'Zoe, are you sure?'

All Zoe could think of was how much she wanted Mitch. Her heart was frantically doing cartwheels; her body was pulsing with desire. He was irresistible. And she didn't want to resist him for a moment longer.

Just one more time. Please. Just one more time with this once-in-a-lifetime man.

She was going into this with eyes wide open, not prompted by fear or anything other than the overwhelming need to have Mitch with her while she had the chance. *One last time.*

'I'm very sure,' she murmured, not even wanting to waste a minute on words when she could be touching instead of talking.

She wound her arms around his neck to kiss him again, parted her lips for his mouth, his tongue, and felt the slide of her dress over her hips as it fell to the floor.

Zoe awoke several hours later. Somehow she was up in her mezzanine bedroom. How…?

She blinked to bring herself to full consciousness. Memories of Mitch carrying her up the stairs to the bed after they'd made love on the sofa filtered through. They'd made love again and she'd fallen asleep in his arms, her head pillowed on his chest, feeling the thud, thud, thud of his heartbeat reverberate through her being as she'd swallowed the words she'd longed to utter: *I love you, Mitch. Don't leave me, Mitch.*

Now she was alone in the bed and she could hear him softly padding around the room. His clothes must be downstairs. She should get up. Go down with him. Watch him as he dressed to leave her and go back to his life that had no room for her. But she couldn't expose herself to that particular form of torture. Instead she drew her knees to her chest and curled her naked self into the tiniest ball possible.

'Zoe? Are you awake?'

She heard his hoarse whisper but she was too weary for words. For platitudes. For promises made in the aftermath of passion and not likely to be kept.

'Mmm…' she murmured, pretending to be asleep.

She felt him stand over the bed. 'I have to go back to my parents' house, Zoe, to pick up my stuff, say goodbye to them. But I'll call around to see you on the way to the airport—around ten. We can say goodbye properly, swap contact details.'

He waited for her answer.

'Okay,' she murmured, hoping she sounded convincingly sleepy.

But when he leaned over to kiss her on the cheek she lost it. Lost all dignity, lost all pride and clung wordlessly to him until he gently unwound her arms and lowered her back onto the bed.

'See you in a few hours,' he whispered, kissing her again before he left.

She held herself rigid in the bed as she listened to him move around downstairs, heard his footsteps walk through the office, the quiet slam of the door closing behind him, the sound of his car disrupting the stillness of the night.

After he'd gone Zoe lay there for a long time, unable to sleep, her thoughts churning round and round. *She couldn't deal with this.* Couldn't allow herself to be picked up and put down at a man's whim.

She wasn't a cool girl—could never be a cool girl able to handle a casual relationship with aplomb. Underneath her stylish clothes and smart haircut she was still Zoe the nerd who longed to be loved.

She didn't want to engage in some battle of the sexes scenario. But it did appear that men were able to make love to a woman—make it seem special and memorable—and then walk away without a backward glance.

As Mitch had done to her in Bali. And had just done again. And she, to save her pride, her heart, had pretended that it didn't hurt.

But to a woman—*this* woman, anyway—it was more difficult to separate sex from emotion. From love. She couldn't just write off an intimate connection like the one she'd just shared with Mitch as a mere physical fling.

She'd been dumb enough to fall in love with him. All he wanted was no-strings fun while she wanted to be bound by ribbons of love and commitment to the man she gave her heart to.

Mitch wasn't that man. He'd made that very clear, much as she might long for it to be otherwise. The lovemaking they'd shared last night had meant nothing to him, though he'd made sure she enjoyed it to the fullest. She'd gone into it willingly. Did not regret it. But she deserved more than Mitch was prepared to give.

Friends with benefits didn't do it for her—no matter how spectacular the benefits.

If Mitch came to see her as promised, later this morning, she would make all the right noises. The *Let's keep in touch*, the *I'll look you up when I'm next in Europe*, the *I hope to see you next time in Sydney*, conversation. But after he left she would wipe Mitch from her mind, from her heart.

At last she dozed off into a fitful sleep. When she awoke again, to early-morning sunlight filtering through the blinds, it was like a repeat of the dreams of him she had suffered since Bali: waking to find she was alone after all. Only this time she could still see where the sheets had twisted around his body, inhale the scent of him, feel the imprint of him on her. He had been only too real.

She got out of bed, staggered with sudden dizziness and a wave of nausea. Coffee. That was what she needed.

She clung to the railing as she made her way down the winding metal stairs that led from the mezzanine to the living area. There was no trace of Mitch left—not even a lingering scent.

Then she saw the toy dog Mitch had won for her, propped on the coffee table. Mitch had joked that he didn't want it watching them and turned its back to them.

Zoe took the few steps over to the coffee table, hugged the fluffy toy to her and let the tears come.

CHAPTER THIRTEEN

AN HOUR LATER Zoe yawned and stretched as she let herself out of her front door. The coffee had done nothing to quell the nausea—in fact just a sip had made it worse. She'd been lucky enough to get a cancellation for an early-morning appointment with her doctor in Balmain village. It was a crisp, sunny morning and she'd decided to walk.

Even after eating only a few bites of her meal last night she'd awoken feeling unwell again. It was annoying to feel like this when she was so used to perfect health. If, as Mitch seemed to think, she had picked up some long-lasting exotic bug she needed to get it fixed. Or maybe it was stress. Or a food allergy. Half the people she knew these days seemed to have some kind of food intolerance.

Then again, maybe it was caused by heartbreak.

She didn't have to wait long to see the doctor. Straight away, Zoe told her how she'd got food poisoning the first day she'd been in Bali and hadn't seemed to get over it. She was astounded when, after listening to her recital of tummy-twisting woes, her doctor suggested she take a pregnancy test.

Zoe shook her head. 'It couldn't be that,' she said. 'I'm on the pill. We were careful. It was only one night.'

Her doctor gave her a reassuring smile as she handed over a pregnancy-testing wand and directed Zoe to the medical practice's bathroom. 'It's a good idea to rule it out for sure.'

Zoe had thought she'd felt fear when the earthquake had hit. But that fear was nothing to what she felt in the privacy of the medical centre's bathroom. She had to wait three endless minutes before she dared to look at the result panel of the testing stick. One thin pink line meant she *wasn't* pregnant. Two pink lines meant she *was* pregnant.

She thought her eyes were blurring when she saw two distinct pink lines. Pink lines as deep in colour as the suit she'd been wearing the day before. She closed her eyes and opened them again, but the two lines were still there. She shook the device, in the hope that it might shake back down to one line, like the mercury in a thermometer. But the two pink lines were still there, glaring at her.

This couldn't be.

Those thin pink lines were turning her life upside down more than any earthquake.

Too numb to move, she stayed a long time in the bathroom. Eventually the practice nurse knocked on the door and asked if she was all right. She staggered back down to the doctor's consulting room, holding on to the corridor wall for support.

'You okay?' her doctor asked.

'Not really,' she said. 'It says I'm pregnant. That's not possible. I…I don't *feel* pregnant.'

But when she really thought about it maybe she did. The off-and-on nausea. Her aversion to certain foods. The inexplicable craving for oranges she'd put down to a need for vitamin C. A tendency to be over emotional, which was not like her at all. And when she'd dressed last night, in that gorgeous purple dress she'd bought just before she went to Bali, she'd been surprised when it had seemed tighter across the bust than she'd remembered.

But her brain refused to accept the possibility.

'Don't I need a blood test to be sure?' she asked.

'The test you've just taken is extremely accurate,' the doctor said. 'But just to be certain I'll ask you to hop up onto the bed so I can examine you.'

Zoe moaned under her breath. Could the day get any worse?

'You're definitely pregnant,' the doctor said, after a series of palpations. 'About eight weeks along, I'd say.'

She was eight weeks pregnant.

It seemed impossible. But the timing was spot-on.

'The sickness you're feeling should start to ease soon, as your hormones settle down,' the doctor said.

'How could this have happened? We took precautions.'

'No precautions are one hundred per cent effective,' the doctor said. 'My guess is that your digestive upset in Bali negated the effectiveness of your pill. Put simply: it wasn't absorbed—it didn't work.'

Zoe squeezed her eyes tight shut. This couldn't be true.

When she opened them it was to see the concerned face of her doctor.

'You have…options…' the doctor said.

'No.' Zoe was stunned by the fierce immediacy of her reply. 'No options. I'm keeping it.'

She couldn't bring herself to say *the baby*. Not yet. Not now.

Mitch's baby.

'The father…?' the doctor probed discreetly.

'We're not…not in a relationship,' Zoe replied. 'I…I'm in this on my own.'

She hardly heard another word as the doctor handed her a bunch of pamphlets. Talked of blood tests. Nutrition advice. Referral to an obstetrician. Choice of hospital. Antenatal classes. Nothing really sank in. This couldn't be happening.

She was going to have a baby in February.

It took her twice as long to walk home as it had to get to the medical centre. Her feet felt leaden and it seemed as if she was walking through dense fog. The more she thought about being pregnant, the more complicated the situation got.

She dreaded telling Mitch. He'd made it so clear he wasn't ready for commitment—certainly not for a family. *'Not until I'm thirty. Maybe thirty-five.'* His words echoed in her head over and over.

Then worse words seeped into her thoughts like poison. Her grandmother. *'I won't have you getting pregnant and ruining the future of some fine young man the way your mother ruined my son's.'*

In Bali she'd told Mitch what her grandmother had said. Was that how Mitch would see it? Would her getting pregnant ruin *his* future? It would certainly change it.

Her breath caught on a half-sob. *Not as much as it would change hers.*

Would he think she'd tried to trap him? That she'd demand money? Even marriage? *The oldest trick in the book.* She couldn't bear to think he would believe that of her.

Imagine if the press got hold of it. How sordid they would make it look. A one-night stand. A holiday fling. A scheming woman. It would not reflect well on him.

Mitch's career was all-important to him. He'd been so clear that he couldn't have distractions at this vital stage of his career. What could be more of a distraction than an unplanned baby—with its mother a woman he was only just getting to know?

A mother. She was going to be a *mother*.

From nowhere came a fierce urge to protect her baby. *Her baby.* This baby would be wanted. Would be loved. This was far from the way she'd dreamed of starting a family, but it had happened. She was strong. She was independent. She could do this on her own.

By the time Zoe got back home she'd made her decision. She would not tell Mitch she was pregnant.

Mitch had an early breakfast with his parents, feeling sad to say goodbye to them while his father was still in a cast and a sling and so obviously in discomfort. But that was another price he paid for his international career—being so far away from his family.

His mother had been determined to drive him to the airport. Much as Mitch loved his mother, he had been equally determined that she would be staying home in Wahroonga. He wanted to drive himself, so he could detour to Balmain and see Zoe one last time before he flew out to Madrid.

As he drove his rental car into Balmain, Mitch realised he was excited—heart-pounding, mind-racing excited—at the thought of seeing Zoe, even for only an hour. He had never felt like this about a woman. Always the game had been first and foremost—his emotions and energy channelled into his relentless drive to the top level.

Realistically, now was not the best time to get involved, to be thinking there might be some kind of future with her. But his attraction to Zoe was as out of his control as the earthquake had been. He had to ride with it.

Their night together had shifted something in his thinking. On the drive back to his parents' house he had found himself wondering if Zoe could play a part in his life. Could she be a support rather than a distraction? Would having her with him in Madrid be less of a distraction than *not* having her there?

Because deep in his gut he knew Zoe was important. *Very* important.

One thing was for sure: he had to see her again, and see her again as soon as possible. Being back in Madrid would be easier if he knew he would be seeing her as soon as they could make it happen. He wanted to make a definite arrangement for her to come and visit as quickly as she possibly could. Her first-class airfare paid by him, of course.

On his third knock, Zoe answered her door.

As a footballer, Mitch was good at reading other players' intentions. Some commentators saw his skill as uncanny. He believed it was because he had been blessed with a well-developed subconscious antennae that picked up on the slightest variations in body language.

But he didn't need more than a basic knowledge of body language to know that something was wrong. Zoe looked washed out and drawn;

her hand braced against the doorframe didn't look steady. His first thought was that she was ill.

'Mitch,' she said, offering her cheek for his kiss, but her greeting wasn't over-burdened with enthusiasm—and certainly not with passion.

He swallowed his dismay. Last night she had been so responsive in his arms.

Today she was wearing skinny black jeans and a loose black top that swamped her slender frame. It drained the colour from her face, making the contrast of her red lipstick appear garish. Her eyes seemed shadowed and dull.

He drew back. Searched her face. 'Are you okay?'

Her gaze slid away from his. 'Just tired. It was such a late night last night.'

Worry for her coursed through him. Fatigue. Illness. *Please don't let there be something seriously wrong with her.*

'You look unwell,' he said, more bluntly than he'd intended.

'I actually went to the doctor this morning,' she said.

'And? Did he test you for tropical bugs?'

'It's not a tropical bug. It's…it's… She's testing me for food allergies.'

'That's great. Not great that it could be an allergy. But great you didn't bring something home from Bali with you.'

Zoe choked, and then started to cough. He patted her on the back until her coughs subsided.

'I'm okay now,' she said.

He frowned. 'I don't like the sound of that cough.'

Her smile was forced. 'There's nothing to worry about. I…I'm not sick.'

Mitch wasn't convinced.

She turned on her spike-heeled black boots. 'It's cold out here. You'd better come in.'

The shiver that went through him had nothing to do with the weather.

Mitch followed her through into her living room. The view was, indeed, as spectacular as he'd thought it would be last night.

'This is a wonderful space,' he said, looking around him.

For the first time she smiled, but it was a wan imitation of her usual smile. 'It is wonderful, isn't it? I get it for a very good rent.'

For the first time Mitch felt an intimation of fear. Was she having second thoughts about them keeping in touch? He regretted not telling her last night that she was so much more to him than a 'friend with benefits'. They'd vaguely discussed her visiting him in Madrid. But nothing concrete. He wanted to remedy that this morning—before he left for the airport.

He looked over to the sofa, where they'd made such passionate love. The cat was firmly ensconced once more, curled up in a ball. It opened one yellow eye, inspected him, and went back to sleep.

'No one working today?' he said. 'Except the mouse-catcher, there, of course.'

His joke about the cat fell flat.

'Louise and our office manager are on a course. I cancelled all my appointments because…'

He wanted her to say it was because he was going to call by and she wanted privacy. But he had a sinking sensation that wasn't what she was going to say.

'Because…because I wasn't feeling well,' she said.

She didn't wait for a reply from him, but turned

away so all he saw of her was her black-clad back. Then she spun round to face him. She crossed her arms in front of her chest, seemed to brace her shoulders.

'I can't do this—with you, I mean,' she blurted out. 'I've thought about it. Not knowing when I'll see you again. Being a...a part-time lover. Sleeping with you with no kind of commitment. It's not me. It...it can only lead to heartbreak—for me, anyway. Why pretend otherwise?'

Mitch was too astounded to answer for a moment. 'I don't get it. Last night we talked about you coming to Madrid.'

'Did we? I don't recall a definite invitation. Just *Drop in for a bootie call if you happen to find yourself in Europe.*'

'Zoe, I didn't meant that.'

But that was exactly what it would have sounded like to her. He cursed under his breath.

'Last night we were kidding ourselves that we could keep something going. But all the barriers are still there and...and they're insurmountable.' Her voice broke.

'I don't agree,' he said. 'We can—'

She put up her hand in a halt sign. 'Don't say it. I've made up my mind. In any case, even if you *were* offering more than friends with benefits, I couldn't deal with the public attention. For a private person like me it would be hell.'

'But last night—'

She spoke over him. 'We…we need to get on with our own lives. I'm sorry, Mitch.'

Her words sounded rehearsed. Was this why she was tired? Had she been up since he'd left here, practising how to dump him?

He fisted his hands by his sides. 'I'm surprised. And disappointed.'

And angry as hell.

'I've thought about it a lot since…since last night.'

'So that's it? It's over between us before it even started?'

Dumbly, she nodded, her eyes bleak.

'Then there's nothing further to be said.'

He turned and walked out. She made no effort to stop him. If she'd been able to read his thought bubbles all that would be visible would be dark, thunderous clouds.

* * *

Mitch was so churned up he was scarcely aware of how he got out of Balmain and on the road to the airport.

What in hell had gone wrong? He couldn't believe Zoe had had such a complete turnaround of feelings.

But he couldn't *make* her feel what he felt— make her see what a good chance they had of something special if they both worked at it.

He had to put her behind him.

It wasn't as if he'd be short of feminine attention once he got back to Madrid.

Oh, yes, there were plenty of eager women around for a player of his standing in La Liga. He was only alone by choice.

But none of them was Zoe.

His hands clenched tightly to the steering wheel. As he drove towards the airport his thoughts spun around and around, unable to make sense of his confrontation with her.

It hadn't seemed right. There had been something about her. She'd seemed...*cowed*. The thought of her face brought back a flash of memory. The way her shoulders had been hunched over, the way she'd kept her eyes to the ground. She'd been like that Zoe he'd wounded long ago in high school.

But he'd done nothing to hurt her this time.

Something else had happened. Something she was hiding from him—for a reason he couldn't fathom.

As he neared the industrial area of Mascot, home to Sydney's Kinsgsford-Smith Airport, he was still puzzling over what he might have missed.

He thought about her doctor's diagnosis. How could the doctor know straight away that Zoe hadn't contracted a tropical disease? There would have to be tests—tests that would take days to come back from a pathologist.

The more he thought about it, the more he was convinced something was seriously wrong. Something Zoe was determined to hide from him.

Twice before she'd left him with unfinished business. The first time when they'd been teenagers. The second in Bali, after a night of passionate lovemaking. There wouldn't be a third time.

He still had a few hours until he had to check in for his flight.

He swung the car around and headed back to Balmain.

CHAPTER FOURTEEN

AFTER MITCH WALKED OUT Zoe was in such a state of shock she couldn't think straight. She immediately began to worry if she had done the right thing in concealing her pregnancy from him.

She hadn't just concealed it—she had *lied* about it. She had out-and-out lied to Mitch by telling him she was being tested for food allergies to explain her symptoms.

Zoe smothered a semi-hysterical laugh. She wasn't very good at deception. She'd always prided herself on her honesty. Mitch must think she was at best unbalanced; she didn't dare think what he might call her at worst. The confusion, hurt and barely suppressed anger on his face at her ill-thought-out words had distressed *her*. Heaven knew how awful it had been for *him*.

She had decided not to continue their friendship before she'd gone to the doctor. But she'd had no intention of blurting it out to him this morning. She just wouldn't have answered his texts, replied to his emails, until he'd got the message. She'd wanted to avoid a messy confrontation.

But that had been before she knew she was pregnant.

She paced the length of the apartment—back and forth, back and forth—totally at a loss to know what to do, until she began to feel dizzy. It seemed surreal that in the space of a few hours her world had been turned so totally upside down, leaving her staggering and disorientated—way worse than after the earthquake.

She'd discovered she was pregnant, and she'd lost Mitch when she'd only just found him.

Finally, when she truly thought she might topple over from a crippling combination of fatigue and angst, she sank into the sofa. Einstein, her dark tabby cat, looked at her with baleful eyes but allowed himself to be hugged tight.

'What am I going to do?' she asked the cat as she stroked him.

The rhythmic motion on his soft fur was soothing to both of them. She often talked to her cat; he was a great listener. It didn't matter that he only answered with the occasional meow that she fancifully imagined to be a reply.

'I'm going to have a human kitten, Einstein, and I don't know how I'm going to cope.'

Her words echoed through the empty space, emphasising her aloneness. Einstein just purred.

In some ways she identified with the cat. He'd been a disreputable-looking stray, hanging around the warehouse complex car park. With patience and cans of tuna she'd tamed him. Once she'd established that he didn't belong to anyone she'd adopted him.

She and Louise had called him Einstein because, as Louise had put it, 'He's a genius cat to have found *you* to dance attendance on him.'

Einstein was as fiercely independent and self-sufficient as Zoe liked to think she was. After all, she was the girl who had emancipated herself from her grandmother aged just seventeen. She'd put herself through university on her own. Got admitted as a chartered accountant. Established her business by herself.

She'd become very good at solving problems without seeking help. But she was totally unprepared for a surprise pregnancy and for bringing up a baby on her own.

Suddenly she was overwhelmed by a fierce longing for her mother. A woman desperately needed her mother with her at a time like this. And her father too. He would have given her good advice on what to do about Mitch.

Should she have told Mitch she was pregnant? Presented it as an issue they needed to look at together? After all, they'd made this baby together. Did he have a right to know he was going to be a father? Was it the wrong thing to do to keep him out of the picture? Should she tell him and make it clear she would make no demands on him—financial or otherwise?

Zoe clutched her head with both hands against the throbbing of an impending headache. Conflicting thoughts and questions she could find no answer to were banking up in her brain and banging to be let out.

She glanced at her watch. It seemed like for ever, but Mitch hadn't been gone long. If she was quick she could catch him on his mobile phone and ask him to come back. Or meet him at the airport.

She didn't have Mitch's number.

They hadn't actually exchanged phone numbers or addresses. There'd been no need to as yet. They'd planned to swap all their contact details this morning, if things had gone differently.

Could she get hold of his number from somewhere? Maybe look up his parents and call them? What kind of reception would she get from his mother? A strange young woman, calling to get her famous soccer star son's personal phone number so she could tell him she was pregnant? As if *that* would happen.

She didn't even have a clue about which airline he was flying with. And no airline would divulge passenger details to tell her if he was booked on their 2:00 p.m. flight to Madrid. If she wanted to talk to him she would have to scurry around the terminal, trying to find him. No way could she bear to do that. If he were flying first class he'd go straight to a private lounge anyway.

It seemed she'd missed her chance to tell him face to face that she was pregnant.

If she decided to tell him at some time in the future she would have to try and contact him in Madrid. Maybe she could find out who was his agent or his manager and get a message to him through them. *Yeah, right.* They'd think she was a groupie or a stalker—or worse.

What a mess she'd made of this.

But she'd had her reasons for not telling Mitch and they'd seemed valid at the time. For the moment she'd stick with them.

Louise would have to be told, though, when she got back at lunchtime. They were good friends as well as work colleagues. Her pregnancy would have implications for the business. It would affect the possible buyout and her plans for expansion. Nothing they wouldn't be able to work through, though. Women got pregnant and managed their careers all the time.

It was Mitch who was her concern.

She sighed and yawned—exhausted, overwhelmed, and weary beyond measure.

'Move over, Einstein,' she said to her cat, so she could stretch out on the sofa beside him.

As she settled herself next to the purring cat at last she allowed herself to think about her baby— the new little person she would be bringing into the world in February. Would she/he look like her and Mitch? Her black hair with his green eyes?

Or a little boy or girl who looked just like Mitch.

She smiled at the thought and put her hand protectively on her still flat tummy. But as she drowsed into sleep she thought about how delighted her mother and father would have been to be grandparents and her smile melted into tears.

Zoe was awoken by an insistent buzzing. She struggled through layers of sleep to recognise it as the front door buzzer. *Please don't let it be a client.* She couldn't even face a delivery person, let alone some number-befuddled artiste who'd got themselves into a huge mess with their tax reporting or their quarterly Business Activity Statement.

Right now she couldn't cope with someone spilling a shoebox full of scrappy invoices and receipts all over her desk and begging for help. Usually she'd see it as a challenge, and be delighted to assist. But today it would be the befuddled leading the befuddled.

She moved a protesting Einstein and swung herself off the sofa. Once on her feet she staggered, and had to steady herself against a sudden light-headedness. With clumsy fingers she pushed her fingers through her hair and rubbed under her eyes for smeared mascara.

'Coming!' she called.

It seemed to take for ever to reach the door, and Zoe took a deep breath before she opened it. She thought she was hallucinating when she saw Mitch standing there. She wiped her eyes with the back of her hand and looked again. But he was still there, as billboard-handsome as ever but with his face set in unfamiliar grim lines.

Mitch.

Joy filtered through her shock to warm her heart. *He'd come back.*

'You're...you're meant to be at the airport,' she managed to choke out.

He didn't explain but rather launched straight into tight-lipped speech. 'Zoe, you obviously have your reasons for saying what you did this morning. But I'm not leaving until I know the truth.'

'I...I wanted to... I didn't have your number and...'

The words seemed to stall in her throat. She stared at him until the lines of his face seemed to go fuzzy. Her hand flew to her mouth. She felt flushed, light-headed, nauseated. She clutched at the doorframe. For the first time in her life she was going to faint.

Zoe felt Mitch catch her, lift her into his arms, cradle her to his chest. She could hear his voice as if it were coming from a long way away.

'Zoe... I've got you, Zoe.'

He carried her to a chair in the waiting area and forced her head between her knees. She was aware of his hand, warm and reassuring on her back.

'Breathe,' he said, his voice coming back into

normal range. 'Breathe in and out, slowly and deeply. You told me you've done yoga. Use your yoga breathing.'

She did as he instructed until the fog cleared. But it was an effort to lift her head.

'Slowly,' Mitch said. 'Lift your head slowly.'

He handed her a paper cup of water from the cooler.

'Just sip it,' he said.

Obediently, she took a few sips of the cold water.

He hunkered down in front of her, his green eyes narrowed. 'Are you going to tell me what's going on?'

Not here. Not now. Not with her at such a disadvantage. She needed her thoughts to be clear.

Weakly, she bowed her head and didn't answer.

'So there *is* something?' he said gruffly.

She nodded.

'I knew it,' he said.

'I…I'm sorry about…this morning…the way I….' She couldn't force the words out. She swallowed hard but it didn't make it any better.

'How long since you've eaten?' he said.

'Last night…I think.'

'When you just nibbled at your dinner? You didn't have any breakfast?'

She shook her head. 'Nothing. I thought the doctor might want to take blood for tests. I didn't want to have to go back another time, so I decided to fast so I could have the tests done straight away.'

It had seemed a good idea at the time. Then, after her visit to the doctor, food had been the last thing on her mind.

'What have you got in your refrigerator? I'll make you something to eat.'

'There's some bread in the freezer. Some toast, maybe?'

'You stay here and keep sipping on that water. Whatever else might be wrong with you, it's my bet you're dehydrated.'

She heard him rattling around in the kitchen. Soon the smell of toast wafted towards her. Suddenly she was starving. But she took Mitch's advice, leaned back in the chair and kept sipping water.

Within minutes he returned, with a plate holding two pieces of wholewheat toast, cut into squares. 'I think you should eat it dry until you see if you can keep it down. Just nibble on it to start with.'

He was so kind. She flushed. What if she didn't keep it down? How humiliating would *that* be in front of Mitch?

But she did keep it down. And she started to feel better. Stronger. Who knew? All she'd needed was some food.

'Thank you so much, Mitch, for looking after me. I feel fine now.' She wasn't used to being pampered—found it difficult to accept it.

'And, from that coolness in your voice, you think you're dismissing me and that I'm going to go away. Not happening. I told you—I'm sticking with you until I get to the bottom of what's going on.'

He'd come back to her.

It changed everything. She would have to pick her moment to tell him the truth. He was every bit as wonderful as she'd thought he was. And more. She would not find it easy to tell him she'd lied to him about something so important. That he was going to be a father.

Mitch was relieved to see the colour return to Zoe's cheeks, the light come back to her eyes. She'd given him a fright by fainting. But it was nothing he couldn't handle. It wasn't uncommon for a player to pass out from the sudden pain and shock of an injury.

Why she'd fainted was what he was determined to know. And why she'd behaved the way she had earlier this morning. It didn't make sense.

At the back of his mind was still the suspicion that there was something very wrong and she was trying to protect him from a painful truth. That was the kind explanation. What he knew for sure was that she was concealing *something* from him.

He didn't give up easily—he would never have got to where he was if he had. He wasn't going to give up on Zoe. Or leave her here to suffer by herself. She had no family. Was so fiercely independent that she wouldn't ask for help from anyone.

He needed to catch that plane and get back to Madrid.

But he'd left her on her own once before, in a corridor at a high school. In all conscience he couldn't to it again.

Who was he kidding? He felt more for Zoe than he ever had for a woman. It would nag at him if he left her—if he didn't look out for her. She awoke in him a deep, almost primeval urge to protect her. He would stay with her, no matter the cost to him.

'You said you'd cancelled your appointments for the day. Is that still the case?' he asked.

She nodded.

'Today's Friday. I assume you don't have any business plans for the weekend?'

'No.'

'Social engagements?'

'None to speak off.'

'Good.'

'What do you mean, "good"?'

'Because I'm taking you away. Somewhere you can get the rest you so obviously need. Somewhere we can talk. Talk until there's no more pretence or prevarication between us. I just need to make a few calls.'

She gripped the arms of the chair. 'You're taking me away? What the heck do you mean by *that*?'

He waved his hand around to encompass her office, the living area, the view to the harbour. 'This isn't working for us. The city. Being in Sydney. It's some kind of barrier. I thought we'd breached it last night. Got back to how we were in Bali. But obviously not.'

'No,' she said softly, looking somewhere near her feet.

'I'm not letting you go without a fight, Zoe. If it were at all possible I'd fly us back to Bali. But that can't happen. So I'm going to take you somewhere else.'

She looked directly up at him. 'You're kidnapping me, Mitch?'

'You could call it that.' She sure as hell wasn't going to get away from him.

Zoe smiled. It was a watery smile, but a smile just the same. 'I think I like the idea of being kidnapped.'

She pushed herself up from her chair. He took her elbow to support her.

'Please don't faint on me again,' he said. 'When your eyes rolled back in your head I thought—'

Those same brown eyes flashed indignation. 'My eyes did *not* roll back in my head.'

'They did.'

'They did not. I would have felt them if they had.'

'Okay, they didn't,' he said, unable to suppress a grin. 'They just...tilted a bit.'

'I don't know whether to take you seriously or not.' She shuddered theatrically. 'That would be such an unattractive look. I wouldn't want you to think of me as an eyes-rolled-back kind of girl.'

'Now I don't know whether to take you seriously or not,' he said.

'You'll never know, will you?' she said, with a challenging tilt to her chin.

She was cute. Very cute. And he was relieved to see a spark of *his* Zoe back again. But he wanted so much more than just a spark. He wanted the Zoe he'd been with in Bali. The Zoe he'd developed feelings for and didn't want to let go.

She frowned. 'But what about Madrid? Shouldn't you be back there? I'm worried that—'

'Let *me* worry about that. I can stretch my absence until Monday. I have to fly out tomorrow evening, come what may, but I'm going to keep you locked up in my kidnapper's lair until tomorrow afternoon. We either sort things out—'

'Or…?'

'Or we say goodbye for good.'

She stood very still. He could hear the ticking of the large clock on the wall behind him, the ding of incoming emails on the computer in the next room, even the faint slap of the water against the wooden piers below the building.

'Okay,' she said at last. 'But I hope you don't intend to gag and bind me and throw me in the back of your car?'

He laughed. She looked so washed out, her eyes shadowed, but that Zoe spirit was still there. 'I wouldn't dare,' he said.

'So…where are you taking me?'

'I can't take you to Bali, so I'm taking you to Palm Beach.'

Her face brightened. 'Palm Beach? I *love* Palm

Beach. Even though I've only ever been there a few times. Even though it's winter.'

'There's a heated pool at the house.'

'I've never been kidnapped before. So what do I pack…?'

'Casual…comfortable. Something warm. It can get chilly by the sea. Oh, and walking shoes.'

Those sexy little boots wouldn't do for long walks on the beach.

He made a few calls on his mobile phone—one of which was to postpone his flight back to Madrid. He had to admire the efficiency with which Zoe packed her small red overnight bag and flung on a black-and-white-checked coat. In less than ten minutes she was ready.

'What about the cat?' he asked.

'I've left a note for Louise. She'll look after him.'

'I'm glad we don't have to take him with us,' he said.

She looked up at him. 'Would you really have brought Einstein with us?' she asked.

'Einstein? You call your cat *Einstein*?'

'Long story. I'll tell you later.'

'Yes. I would have brought Einstein with us if I'd had to. I don't mind cats.'

She went very quiet again. 'We haven't even established whether we like dogs or cats yet, let alone—'

'We can talk about that on the way down to the beach,' he said. 'Though, for the record, I love dogs and I like cats too. We had both when I was growing up. Not having a dog or a cat around the place is one of the things I miss, living in Spain.'

But they didn't get a chance to talk about dog and cats, or favourite movies or their taste in music, let alone the reasons Zoe had stonewalled him earlier this morning.

Because almost as soon as he'd driven the car out of Balmain and over the Anzac Bridge, heading north to the Harbour Bridge, Zoe had fallen asleep.

CHAPTER FIFTEEN

ZOE WAS ANNOYED with herself to find she had slept for most of the one-hour drive to Palm Beach—the most northern of Sydney's northern beaches. Her time with Mitch was so limited, and she didn't want to waste a minute of it.

But by the time her eyes had started to flicker open they had already driven past every one of the long, sandy beaches and the surrounding suburbs that lay between Manly and Palm Beach.

By the time her eyes were fully open they were on Barrenjoey Road, with the blue, boat-studded waters of Pittwater on their left, and cruising into Palm Beach. She barely had time to notice the handful of shops and restaurants that formed the hub of this exclusive, resort-like suburb as they flashed past.

Zoe didn't know how many times she'd heard Palm Beach referred to as 'the playground of the rich and famous'. When Hollywood celebrities jetted into Sydney in the summer it was often to stay in luxurious beach houses owned by themselves or their billionaire Aussie friends up here on the Barrenjoey Peninsula. Real estate was prized on this strip of land that jutted out into the sea, bounded by the surf beach on one side and the calm waters of Pittwater on the other.

Still feeling a tad drowsy, she allowed herself the luxury of watching Mitch as he drove. He made even an everyday thing like driving a car look graceful and controlled. Both hands were firmly on the wheel as he concentrated on the road ahead. She noticed he wore one of the expensive watches he endorsed in an advertising campaign. He'd told her he only endorsed products he believed were of the best quality and design. His face—already so familiar to her—was set in such a serious expression. Designer sunglasses masked his eyes.

She wished she could see his thought bubbles. Was he looking ahead to a future—if his knee continued to hold up—as an elite athlete at the top of his field?

He was a determined, driven man who had made his thoughts about not settling down until he was in his thirties very clear. And yet it appeared he was serious about wanting her as part of his future in some way—he wouldn't have turned around at the airport otherwise.

But it wasn't just about *her* now—or even about *him*. They'd made a baby together. The way he'd looked after her when she'd fainted gave her cause to think that despite his celebrity status he was not the kind of man who would deny his own child. *He would make a good father.* It would be up to her to make sure he played some role in their child's life.

'That trip went fast,' she said, trying out her voice and finding it to be back to normal. She had never, ever fainted before.

'The lady awakes,' Mitch said, giving her a sideways glance.

Zoe remembered waking up next to him in Bali, after a night of sensual pleasure. How wonderful that time together had been—as it had been last night. She longed to be something more in his life and not to have to say goodbye in the morning. Would it ever happen?

'I missed the whole drive down. I wish you'd woken me up,' she said.

He smiled. 'So you could quiz me about my preference for dog over cat?'

'Something like that.' She'd planned to segue into his thoughts on having kids.

'You obviously needed the sleep,' he said. 'Feeling any better?'

'Much better,' she said, stretching her limbs as best she could in the confines of the car. 'Thank you.'

'We're nearly there,' he said.

'So I see.'

It was a magnificent winter's day, the sky cloudless, the sea a deep blue.

'It's ages since I've been down here. I'm a city girl—I don't stray over the bridge too often.'

'We came down here for a couple of vacations when I was a kid and I loved it. A friend of my parents had a house here.'

'Nice,' she said.

Now the road ran parallel to the surf beach that stretched to the Barrenjoey headland at one end and Whale Beach at the other. Even on a week-day in winter there were people swimming, and others in wetsuits, riding boards or paddling surf kayaks out into the breakers.

She opened her window to enjoy the salty air.

'We lived in Newtown,' she said. 'My parents weren't much for the outdoor life. They were arty, musical, and preferred to hang out in coffee shops rather than on beaches. Though when I was older I went with friends to the eastern suburbs beaches, like Bondi and Coogee. That was…that was before I moved to Wahroonga.'

'I was always a north shore boy. I learned to surf here, how to handle a surf kayak. My brothers were older than me—they taught me.'

'Knowing you, you probably overtook them at it your first day in the water.'

'Yeah. That's how it happened. They weren't too happy, having their kid brother beating them so quickly. But that was the way it was in my family. I was the brawn—they were the brains. And that's how it's played out. Just like my parents planned—they got a doctor, a lawyer and a banker.'

'And one of the best sportsmen in the world,' she reminded him.

'They appreciate that—don't worry. They're very proud of my success. They always supported me in anything I wanted to do,' he said.

'But why did they pigeonhole you?' she said, indignant on his behalf.

'They recognised our aptitudes early on, I suppose.'

'You've got plenty of brains. I know that for sure. You even ended up writing a halfway decent piece of poetry for that last essay.'

'You mean the essay that got the big red "fail"?' he reminded her.

'I don't know how that awful teacher could have thought you had plagiarised that poem,' she said.

'You mean because it was so very, very bad?' he said with a grin.

'It wasn't bad. She just didn't appreciate the analogy between scoring goals in a soccer game and goals in life. It was wonderfully rich in similes and metaphors and—'

'And more similes and metaphors, and a whole heap of words I didn't understand. It was *bad*, Zoe,' he said. 'Admit it.'

'It didn't have to be a masterpiece to get you a pass,' she said. 'I liked it, and that's that.'

He glanced sideways at her. 'Thank you for your loyalty. I didn't deserve it.'

She put up her hand in a halt sign. 'No need to go there again.'

She wondered how loyal he would feel towards *her* when she told him she was pregnant.

'I got a place to study engineering at the University of New South Wales. Did I tell you that?'

'You didn't—that's fantastic. You must have done well in the final exams.'

'I had no intention of taking up the place, of course,' he said. 'To play football was all I'd ever wanted to do since my grandfather took me to my first game at White Hart Lane in London. I applied to university just to prove I could get in.'

At the south end of the beach Mitch turned off and swung into a street a few hundred metres back from the water. He pulled up in the driveway of an elegantly simple house, rising to two storeys, all whitewashed timber and huge windows. It was surrounded by perfectly groomed tropical gardens. In an area of multi-million-dollar houses, it fitted right in.

'Is this your parents' friends' house?' Zoe asked. 'It's fabulous.'

'No, it's mine,' he said simply.

'Oh,' she said, not attempting to hide her surprise. Mitch hadn't mentioned owning property of any kind. But then she hadn't asked.

He opened her car door and went around to swing out both her small bag and one of his own.

'This house looks like a very posh kidnapper's lair,' she said.

'I don't think you'll object too much to the conditions of captivity,' Mitch replied with a smile.

They took a small glass-fronted elevator from the garage to the second floor. Zoe stepped into an airy, spacious living room that opened out through folding glass doors to a deck and an infinity edge swimming pool. Beyond that was a magnificent view of the sea, right up to the Barrenjoey headland, filtered by a stand of the tall cabbage palm trees that gave the area its name.

She turned to Mitch. 'Can you forgive me if I can't come up with anything more than *wow*?' she said. 'Except maybe *wow* again? I could look at that view all day.'

'I bought the house for the view.'

'The house itself isn't too shabby either,' she said.

The interior looked as if it had been designed by a professional, in tones of white with highlights of soft blue and bleached driftwood. Large artworks with abstract beach and marine life themes were perfectly placed through the room. It was contemporary and stylish, straight from the pages of a high-end decorating magazine. And yet there were homey touches everywhere—like a shabby-chic old pair of oars, a glass buoy covered in ancient knotted rope, tiny wooden replicas of fishing boats—that took away any intimidating edge.

What an idyllic place for children.

She slipped off her coat. The sun streaming through the windows made it superfluous.

'The house is awesome, isn't it?' said Mitch. 'I bought it with all the furniture included when the market was down, for a very good price.'

Zoe's money-savvy brain recognised that he'd got a good deal by buying at the right time. But around here a 'very good price' would still measure in the multi-millions.

Great. Just great. Mitch must be very wealthy. Wealthier than she'd thought he must be. And, from her experience with her clients, the wealthier they were, the more protective they were of their money—and defensive against people they suspected of wanting to take a bite out of it.

Like a girl who got pregnant on a holiday fling and came looking for a pay-out.

She forced the negative thought to the back of her mind. If she wasn't to tie herself up in knots of anxiety again she had to trust in Mitch that he wouldn't believe she'd had any other motive that night in Bali than to be with him. No matter what else he might come to believe when she told him about her visit to the doctor.

'Let me show you around,' Mitch said.

He took her for a quick tour. The kitchen seemed to be stocked with every appliance and piece of equipment possible. The bathrooms were total luxury. Each of the four bedrooms had ocean views.

Mitch took her overnight bag to the master bedroom, with its enormous bed and palatial en-suite bathroom. 'I'm putting your bag in here,' he said.

She stilled. 'And where are you putting yours?' she asked.

'That's up to you,' he said.

Whatever happened here in this beautiful house, whatever transpired with Mitch, she didn't want to sleep in a different bedroom from him.

'Put your bag with mine. Here. Please.'

The bedroom opened up onto a balcony. While Mitch went to get his bag she stepped out onto the balcony, breathed in the salt air. A flock of multi-coloured lorikeets took flight from the orange flowering grevillea that grew next to the pool. This truly was a magnificent place.

Mitch placed his bag next to hers and came up behind her on the balcony. He put his arms around her and pulled her back to rest against his chest. After a split second of hesitation she let herself relax against his solid strength. She felt safe, secure—and terrified.

This. Mitch. His arms wrapped around her, his breath stirring her hair, his powerful body close. It was what she wanted. Now. And in the future. She was terrified that would never happen. Not when he discovered how dishonest she'd been with him.

That she was pregnant.

* * *

Mitch held Zoe close, relieved she hadn't pushed him away. He didn't want to let her go. Out of his arms—out of his life. They had twenty-four hours to sort out whatever was troubling her. He just hoped it was something he could work with—or solve for her.

He wanted her with him.

The more he was with her, the more he realised that a 'now and then' relationship wouldn't satisfy him for long. What he felt for her couldn't be blocked or passed or sent off the pitch.

'A good substitute for Bali?' he asked as they both looked ahead at the view.

'Oh, yes,' she said. 'It must be glorious in summer.'

'One day, maybe, I'll get to see it in summer. Usually I don't even get back to Australia for Christmas.'

'So you bought the house as an investment?'

'An investment for now. A home for later. When my football career is over.'

He hated to say those words. Right now he couldn't bear even to think about a life without playing.

'Is that inevitable?'

'It's a young man's game. I've still got good years ahead of me.' If the knee stood up to it. And if he didn't suffer any other serious injuries. 'But, yes. It will end.'

'What do you plan to do? Afterwards, I mean?'

Mitch liked it that Zoe didn't seem to realise he would never have to work again. He'd been careful with investments and he would continue to be. That was where banker and lawyer brothers came in handy.

'I was bored witless while I was recuperating,' he said. 'I had a good look into some of the injury prevention devices for sportsmen. Shin guards, ankle wraps, mouth guards. That kind of thing. I reckon they could be better. I'm looking into that.'

'Sounds good. You'd still be involved in sport.'

'But that all seems a long way away, Zoe. I don't want to think about it too much. I'm concerned about the now, not the future.'

'Of course,' she murmured, her voice subdued.

The change in her tone signalled a warning. They had limited time. He had to try and rec-

reate the atmosphere that had brought them together in such a spectacular way back in Bali at
her villa.

'I can't promise roosters.'

'Just parrots?' she said.

'Or Indonesian food,' he said.

'Or earthquakes?' she added.

Mitch could think of various ways he might
make the earth move for her, as he had last night.
He could carry her right now to that big bed behind them in the bedroom. But first he had to
find out why she had behaved the way she had
this morning. After the fun they'd had at Luna
Park, after the lovemaking they'd shared, he still
wondered why she had dismissed him so coldly.

'However, there *is* a swimming pool—that's
bigger and better than the one at the villa.'

'With colder water?' she said pretending to
shiver.

He looked over to the sparkling blue pool.
There was no elephant in residence. Both he and
Zoe knew what had to be tackled.

'The water should be heated up enough to

swim,' he said. 'Not quite the same as Bali, but warm enough.'

'It's the most beautiful pool—I've never swum in a wet edge pool before. Are you sure I won't drift over the edge?'

He laughed. 'There's a ledge below. It's quite safe. Anyway, I'm here to catch you if you get into trouble,' he said.

'Are you, Mitch?' she said, in that tremulous voice that worried him.

She went to ease away from him but he hugged her tighter. 'Of course I am.'

They stood without speaking for a long moment.

Zoe broke the silence. 'So. The pool. Do you leave the heating on all the time?'

'The pool is solar-heated. But there's a gas-fired booster. I called the manager this morning and got her to switch it on.'

'You have a manager?'

'She looks after several of the properties here for absentee owners. My family use the house too. And sometimes I let it out to carefully vetted guests.'

'That makes sense. If the house is earning income you can get tax benefits too.'

'Of course you *would* know that,' he said. 'I also got the manager to stock the fridge with basics.'

'I was wondering about that. I wasn't sure what kidnappers did about feeding their victims. And it's been a while since that toast. It must be lunchtime.'

'Some of the restaurants here do delivery service. I asked the manager to pick up their latest menus.'

'So we can get room service? Like in Bali?'

'Yes,' he said. 'We can order lunch now.'

Zoe twisted in his arms so she faced him. He refused to let her go.

'Mitch, before we order lunch, and definitely before I get into a bikini, there's something I have to tell you.'

Mitch held his breath. *What was coming?*

She looked up at him, her eyes huge in her wan face.

'I'm pregnant.'

CHAPTER SIXTEEN

MITCH COULD NOT BELIEVE what he was hearing. *Zoe was pregnant?* He gently pushed her away from him. Stared at her as if he she were a stranger as he tried to process what she had just told him. Then the reality of it hit him. He cursed loud and hard.

How had he let this happen? He had trusted her. What an idiot he had been to lose control in Bali. Not to take absolute charge over contraception. What the hell had he got himself into?

Damn. Damn. *Damn.*

She didn't say another word, just stood on the veranda facing him, the glorious view stretching behind her. He knew she was nervously waiting for his response, but he was too shocked to say anything. Nothing in his twenty-seven years had prepared him for this moment. He cursed again.

He didn't know a lot about pregnant women—in fact he knew virtually nothing. He hadn't been in Australia when his nephews—the children of his oldest brother and his wife—had been born.

But some of the cards began to fall into place. Sickness, fainting, fatigue—all symptoms of a worrying serious illness. *Or a pregnancy.* What a blind fool he'd been.

'You're pregnant? And you didn't tell me?'

She flinched at the harshness of his voice but he didn't care. He'd been so careful to protect his future. Now a moment's lust, a moment's carelessness, had thrown everything off course.

She didn't look any different—still slim. But when he thought about last night he remembered that her breasts had seemed larger. He'd appreciated that. It must be a symptom too.

'I only found out myself this morning,' she said.

Her bottom lip was quivering, and she looked near to tears, but she met his gaze fearlessly. She gripped the veranda railing so hard her knuckles showed white.

'This morning? When you went to the doctor?' Strangely, he believed her.

'Yes. I got the shock of my life,' she said. 'I wasn't expecting it at all.'

He looked again at her slender figure in the tight black jeans. 'You're absolutely sure you're pregnant?'

She nodded. 'There's no doubt. The doctor gave me a test and examined me.'

Zoe pregnant.

He was struggling to get his head around it.

'But how did it happen?' He realised what a stupid remark that was the second the words were out of his mouth. He and Zoe had made love with passionate intensity all through that sizzling tropical night two months ago.

Through her misery, a spark of *his* Zoe emerged. 'The usual way,' she said. 'You know—basic biology.'

'But we were careful. You're on the pill.' He ran a hand through his hair in frustration. He should have taken care of the contraception.

'I know. But the doctor told me the pill doesn't work if it's not absorbed. And the Bali belly meant it didn't get digested. So no protection.'

It was the first time Mitch had seen Zoe so

downcast; her lovely mouth set tight, her face strained, her eyes shadowed.

'So your illness wasn't an illness at all?'

'The initial food poisoning, yes. But once I got back to Australia it was what's called morning sickness.' Her mouth twisted wryly. 'Or, in my case, sometimes all-day sickness.'

Percolating through Mitch's shock was real anger. He'd been worried half-crazy about her. Driving back from the airport earlier, he had been imagining her with a serious, possibly fatal illness. What angered him was how dishonest she'd been.

He'd been stupid. She'd lied.

He made no effort to mask his anger. 'So when did you intend to tell me you were pregnant?'

He doubted she was even aware she was wringing her hands together. 'I…I didn't know how you would react. What…what you'd think of me.'

'You were going to let me fly back to Madrid without a word? What was I going to get—a lawyer's letter, demanding maintenance?'

She cringed from him. 'No! I was in shock. I was…frightened.'

Mitch took a step towards her. 'You were *frightened*? Frightened of *me*? What did you think I would do to you?'

Her face crumpled. 'I didn't know. I was so shocked. Trust me when I say it never entered my head that I could be having a baby. I didn't want you to think I…I'd tricked you into…into some kind of commitment. Or that I expected anything from you. I know how important it is to you to be…unencumbered. A baby certainly doesn't figure anywhere in your plans.' Her chin rose. 'It didn't figure in mine either.'

A baby. The actual word 'baby' hit him. Pregnancy was one thing. Baby was another. The reality was that Zoe was bearing a child—*his* child. Realising that sent Mitch into a deeper state of shock.

He and Zoe were going to be parents.

'Did you *ever* intend to tell me that I was going to be a father?'

He a father. Zoe the mother of his child.

The thoughts were so shocking, so unexpected, whirling around his head.

'Yes. No. I didn't know what to do.'

'You lied to me, Zoe. You said your sickness was caused by food allergies.'

'It was the first thing I could think of that might sound plausible. I didn't want you going back to Madrid worrying about it. Not when I know how extremely important the next few months are for you.'

'You're damn right about that,' he said.

Her chin tilted. 'I don't expect anything from you, Mitch. Not money. Not support.' Her mouth twisted bitterly. 'I know I'm nothing to you except a casual bedmate. If I ever thought anything else this sure as heck proves it.'

She headed for the bedroom, pushing past him. She picked up her red bag.

'I assume I can get a taxi from here? I'll walk down to the surf club to wait for one.'

He took a step towards her. 'Zoe—stop.'

She put a hand up to ward him off. 'Don't come near me,' she said, her voice as cold as her eyes.

She was leaving him again.

He grabbed her arm. She went still.

'Touch me again, Mitch, and I'll have an assault charge on you so fast your head will be spinning.'

He stared at her, shocked. How had it come to this? After all they'd shared last night? What had happened to his plans for her to become part of his life? He'd been wrong to react the way he had.

She turned and walked away from him, her back ramrod-straight. But he could see her shoulders shaking.

As she left the room the enormity of what he'd done hit him. Zoe hadn't planned this. She'd tried to save him worry. He cared for her. *She was having his child.* And she was walking out of his life. A life he'd begun to hope she could share with him.

He took the strides necessary to reach her. 'Zoe. Stop. I'm sorry. I was out of order, speaking to you in that way. It was a shock. But I was wrong to react like that.'

She turned back to face him, her lips set in a tight line. 'I want nothing from you, Mitch.'

'But what about the baby?'

'There's just one thing. For his or her sake I'd like you to acknowledge the child as yours. To play a role in its life.'

The truth slammed into Mitch and left him reeling. *He wanted Zoe. He wanted the baby.*

'Zoe, I really am sorry. Please don't walk away. It was an accident, but we're in it together. *My* child. *My* responsibility. You don't have to go through this by yourself.'

To his intense relief she put down her red bag.

No way was he going to 'play a role' in his son or daughter's life. He was going to be a father. A *good* father. Like his father had been to him. And his grandfather before him.

'When is the baby due?'

'February, the doctor said.'

The reality of it hit him with full force. Something akin to anticipation, even a stirring of excitement, began to infiltrate his thoughts.

'My parents will be beside themselves,' he said. 'Especially my mother—she's desperate for more grandchildren.'

'You...you'd tell your *parents*?' Zoe's eyes were huge with trepidation.

'Of course I'll tell my parents. This isn't just about you and me, Zoe. Not any more. This will be the next generation of my family. A Bailey grandchild. A Bailey great-grandchild. A niece or nephew. A cousin. In my family our child will be a reason for celebration—not commiseration.'

Zoe shook her head in seeming disbelief. She put her hand on her belly in an age-old gesture of protection that shot straight to Mitch's heart.

'I…I'm still coming to terms with this. That we've made a little person.'

'You're thinking about what your grandmother said, aren't you?'

That mean old witch had a lot to answer for, the way she'd treated her hurting, vulnerable granddaughter. She wouldn't be getting her claws into *his* child, that was for sure.

Mutely, Zoe nodded.

'This baby won't ruin my life,' Mitch said. '*You* are not ruining my life. We're twenty-seven—not seventeen. Our careers are established. We've got more than enough money.'

Zoe had no idea just how much money.

'All true,' she said.

But Mitch could sense a big Zoe *but* coming up.

The more he thought about this baby, the more

he thought it wasn't such a disaster. He wanted Zoe. He had to look after her and the baby. They had to be with him.

'Zoe,' he said. 'Come here.'

He held out his arms to her. Her eyes widened but she took the few steps needed so he could draw her into his arms. He held her tight, close to his heart. He allowed relief to flood through him. She was okay. Not ill. Not terminal. *Pregnant with his child.* He would look after her. He would protect her.

'I'm not angry. Not any more,' he said. 'I'll admit it was a shock. But this child is our responsibility. We need to get married as soon as possible.'

Zoe froze in Mitch's arms. She pulled away. Looked up at him. 'Get *married*?'

Mitch drew his brows together. 'Of course, get married. You're pregnant.'

He sounded so certain, so matter-of-fact.

Problem solved. Let's get on with it.

Not a word about love.

Could you actually feel a heart breaking? That

must surely be the explanation for the sudden pain that stabbed her somewhere in that region.

During those long, sleepless hours this morning, when she'd decided to end things with Mitch, she'd allowed herself a single moment to dream of the impossible. She'd let herself fantasise that Mitch would fall in love with her the way she'd fallen in love with him. That their planets might end up permanently aligned.

Her pregnancy had put paid to those dreams.

Those ever-present tears started to sting her eyes again but she fiercely blinked them back. *Darn hormones.*

'Just because I'm pregnant it's no reason to get married,' she said.

Mitch's frown deepened. 'Of course it is. I'm old-fashioned, Zoe. I want us to be married before you have the baby.'

She broke away from him, turned, looked blindly out at the view. Then spun back to face him.

'Mitch, I appreciate your gesture. It's honourable of you. Gentlemanly. But I can't marry you.'

'I don't get it. You're having my child. I want it

to have my name. I want us to be together when he or she is born. To bring our child up together. Give him or her a good life.'

'That's impossible.'

He shrugged. 'There'd be some logistical problems—I acknowledge that. You'd have to come to Madrid to live with me. I can't live here. Not now. Not yet. But I know you want to travel, learn European languages, so I hope you won't mind that. We'd have to sort something out with your business... You could even bring your cat if you wanted.'

The pain in her heart intensified. She wanted to be with Mitch in Madrid more than anything—but not like this.

'No, Mitch. I can give my child a good life here in Sydney. But I want my child to know his or her father. I want you to be involved. Maybe... maybe when our baby is older he or she could spend time with you in Madrid, or wherever you end up living. It should be possible to have some kind of shared custody, if that's what you want. I don't know... I haven't had time to think it through.'

If only it could be different—him, her and their baby together.

Mitch's mouth set in a hard line. For the first time she saw the toughness, the aggressive strength she knew must be there for him to have got where he was in his ultra-competitive world.

'I don't agree,' he said. 'A child needs both mother *and* father, and I want to be a father to my child.'

'You *can* be a father, Mitch. I would encourage you to have a relationship with our child. I...I just don't want to get married.'

How it hurt to say that. *To lie.*

'Why, Zoe? Surely it's the only answer.'

Slowly, she shook her head. 'Mitch, I don't think I'm getting through to you.' It was difficult to keep her voice steady and reasoned. 'Don't you remember what I told you in Bali? I only want to get married if...if I'm head over heels in love.'

'I remember,' he said slowly.

The love was there on her side. There was no doubt about that. She'd been in love with him when she was seventeen—a hopeless, unrequited love. And it had been ignited again in Bali, she now realised.

'The man I marry has to love me in the same way. I…I can't settle for less. Not…not even to give my baby its father's name.'

'But, Zoe, I *do* love you,' Mitch said.

Her poor wounded heart soared. But she yanked it firmly back to the ground again.

'Mitch, you don't have to say that. It doesn't change things.'

Mitch took her by the shoulders, his voice low and urgent. 'Zoe, I'm not just saying this. I *love* you. Why do you think I came back this morning? Brought you down here? You know I'll get a hell of a fine and a reprimand from my club for not being on that plane to Madrid, for missing a game.'

'You're missing a *game*? But, Mitch, that's so important to you. Your knee—your—'

'Not as important as you, Zoe. When I drove home from your place last night I was determined you'd come and visit me in Madrid as soon as you could. Once you were there, I might not have been able to let you go. I'm asking you to marry me now. Most likely I would have asked you to marry me when you came to Madrid.'

'But it… But… I want to believe you, but it seems so sudden.'

'Does it?' He tilted her face so she was forced to meet his gaze. 'I wasn't completely honest with you in Bali.'

She shrank back from him. 'What do you mean?'

'I left out part of my story about when we were at school together. When I came back from soccer camp I kept looking out for you at school because I wanted to say how sorry I was for the way I'd behaved. But that wasn't all. I missed you. *Really* missed you. School wasn't the same without you. I missed our talks. I missed the way we laughed together. The way you believed I was so much more than anyone else thought I was.'

'I still think that,' she murmured, not expecting an answer.

'When I went round to your grandmother's place and she told me you wouldn't be coming back I was gutted. I got moody—bad-tempered. Lara didn't like it. "What's the matter with you?" she taunted me. "Were you in love with that geek girl?"'

Zoe felt herself blush for her seventeen-year-old self. 'Surely she didn't say that?'

'She'd hit on a truth I hadn't recognised until she put voice to it. It all made sense. I *did* have feelings for you—feelings I hadn't acknowledged. That's why I missed you so much. I snapped back at Lara. Denied it. I realised then why she'd been so mean to you. She was jealous. She'd seen how it was with you and me from the get-go.'

'I can't believe this,' Zoe said, slowly shaking her head. She wanted to believe it. But it seemed surreal.

'Believe it,' said Mitch. 'My first break-up with Lara was over you.'

'But you got back with her. Stayed with her for years, on and off.'

'You weren't around. I was seventeen. Lara was persuasive. What can I say?' Mitch said with a rueful grin.

'So how do you explain what happened in

Bali?' she said, still reeling from what Mitch had confessed.

'You caught my eye straight away. I thought you were hot even before I recognised you.'

'Really?' she said, pleased. It didn't hurt a plain girl's ego to hear that she'd caught Mitch Bailey's eye.

'You were wearing a towel that scarcely covered your amazing body. Of *course* I noticed you.'

'I don't know what to say to that,' she said. 'I was terrified the towel was going to fall off.'

'I was hoping the towel *would* fall off.'

'Mitch!' she said with mock indignation, and laughed.

'I thought I was long over you. That my feelings for you had been a teen thing. I was glad to see you and to be able to put things straight. That was all. I didn't expect to fall in love with you all over again.'

'And…did you?' She couldn't control the tremor in her voice.

He nodded with a smile that set her heart racing. 'But I didn't realise how hard I'd fallen until

I was back in Madrid. I tried to deny it. *Man*, did I try to deny it. The timing wasn't right. Like the timing of this baby isn't right. But we can't control that, can we? Life can have a way of making up our minds for us.'

'My getting pregnant, you mean? Or...or you falling in love?'

'Both,' he said. He cupped her face in his strong, gentle hands. 'What about you, Zoe? Could you fall in love with me?'

The look of mingled hope and expectation in his eyes made her knees feel weak and shaky.

'Oh, Mitch, I'm already in love with you.'

'Head over heels?'

'So head over heels I feel dizzy. I had a crush on you at school, but I never dreamed it would be reciprocated in any way.'

'It was such a long time ago. We were kids.'

'But the emotions were real,' she said slowly. She thought back to those hours she'd spent with Mitch in the privacy of her villa. 'I...I think I fell in love with you during our water fight.'

'I can't pinpoint when. It was just...*there*,' he said. 'And everything changed. I tried to tell myself it was just a vacation thing. Reaction to fear of the earthquake. All that. Then when I saw you in Sydney, looking so hot in that pink suit, I knew the attraction was genuine. But you were so glamorous, so contained—so unlike the Zoe I'd known in Bali. I wasn't sure it was the same person.'

'I was terrified of saying the wrong thing. It took a while for us to relax with each other.'

'Yes,' he said. 'Until I wiped you out on the dodgems.'

'I'm glad we worked it out,' she said, hoping he could tell the depth of her feelings for him.

At last he kissed her, his mouth warm and possessive and tender.

Kissing a man you loved, who loved you, who wanted to spend his life with you, felt so different from the other kisses she'd shared with Mitch. Just as exciting, just as sensual, but taken to a new level by love. She wanted Mitch's kisses for the rest of her life. Never anyone else's.

There never had been anyone else, she realised. This was true love—first love.

And they were going to have a baby. A little

boy or girl to bring more joy and love into their lives.

She pictured a little boy who looked just like Mitch, kicking a soccer ball around with his father's skill and talent. Or a little girl doing the same thing. A little girl with her dark hair and—

She broke the kiss 'Mitch, one little thing…'

'Yes?' he said.

'You know how you didn't recognise me at first?'

'It didn't take long. You were still the same Zoe. You just looked a bit different. Your hair, your—'

'My nose. I had a nose job when I was twenty-one. I thought I should let you know that. Just in case the baby… Well, the baby won't inherit this expensive new nose. The old one is still there, lurking in my genes. With a horrid bump in the middle.'

Mitch laughed. He gently stroked down her nose with his finger. 'This is a very nice nose. But I never even noticed you had a bump in it before.'

He kissed her again, deep and slow. She looked

over his shoulder at that big, imposing bed. It would only take a few steps to take them there.

Mitch broke away from the kiss. His breathing was heavier, his eyes a shade darker with desire.

'So, will you marry me, Zoe?'

She didn't hesitate. 'Oh, yes, Mitch. *Yes.*'

They kissed for a long, long time. Then Mitch started to walk her back into the bedroom.

She broke the kiss to murmur against his mouth. 'Do you want to know what's in my thought bubbles?'

'Yes,' he said.

'No words. They're just filled with beautiful rainbows of joy,' she said.

CHAPTER SEVENTEEN

The following June

ZOE LEANED FORWARD in her VIP seat in the president's box of the Madrid stadium, where the final game of the Spanish La Liga season was being played at the home of Mitch's club. They only needed to draw to win the league and become the champions—the most sought-after of honours.

Mitch was below on the pitch, playing the toughest and most important game of his career to a packed stadium of nearly one hundred thousand spectators.

She could only imagine how it had felt for him as he had run through the players' tunnel onto the pitch to be greeted by the mighty collective roar of the fans. The game was being beamed worldwide by satellite to millions more fans—maybe billions.

Mitch, the only Australian, had become a star in a star-studded team. Over the course of the season that had been a test of his injured knee, he had scored ten goals in a total of twenty-seven league games—the best of his career.

But now the vast stadium was silent as, in the dying seconds of the game, her husband lined up to take the free kick that would decide the outcome of the game against his team's closest rival.

Five of the opposition's players had lined up to form a wall, each of them with their hands cupped over their nether regions for protection against a possible hit by the ball.

At any other time Zoe would have found that action amusing. But not now. Her fingernails were digging into her hands so hard they were drawing blood, but she didn't notice.

All she was aware of was Mitch as he took the free kick and curled the ball up over the heads of the players in the wall and into the top corner of the net. It was a breathtaking demonstration of his skill that left the goalkeeper helpless.

Goal!

Zoe jumped up from her seat, fists pumping in the air, as she cheered for her husband. He had scored an equalising goal to clinch the title for his team. *They'd won the league!* Mitch's team were now the champions—the most important title for any major club.

The crowd erupted into a deafening roar of approval.

On the large-screen monitor she saw a close-up of Mitch's face, his expression one of triumphant ecstasy, his grin huge. He acknowledged the crowd's cheers and pulled off his team shirt, leaving his perfectly sculpted chest bare as, arms outstretched, he ran a victory lap in only his shorts and long white socks. He looked breathtakingly handsome and the fans went delirious.

Then he was overtaken by his jubilant teammates in a great show of hugging and back-slapping that culminated in the players throwing their grinning coach above their heads in the air.

Part of the gig of being married to a soccer star was that Zoe had to share his bare chest with the world. There were internet video channels dedicated to just that—shots of Mitch with his shirt off. But she had to deal with it, knowing that while Mitch might be public property to his fans he came home to share *her* bed and enjoy the private family life they cherished. He had never given her cause not to trust him implicitly.

She looked down to where baby Isabella still slept in the carrycot by her feet, oblivious to her famous daddy's triumph.

Zoe's heart seemed to flip over with love for her daughter. Mitch called her the most beautiful baby in the world. With her mummy's dark hair, her daddy's green eyes and straight nose, she was very pretty. Her sweet nature and bright ways made her a joy to have in their lives. If she would just learn to sleep through the night Bella—as she was already called—would indeed be perfect.

It remained to be seen if she would grow up to be the soccer star her father predicted she would be.

In the next seat to her Amanda Bailey, Mitch's mother, wiped away tears of pride in her youngest son. She looked dotingly on her only female grandchild.

'The little pet didn't stir—even with all that commotion,' she said.

Zoe met Amanda's eyes in a perfect communication of shared joy. From being initially wary of Zoe, Amanda had become the best mother-in-law Zoe could ever have imagined having.

Even though they had at first questioned the haste of their son's wedding plans, Mitch's parents had come up trumps in helping them organise the ceremony and reception at short notice.

The ceremony had been perfect—held in the small chapel of an ancient monastery just outside of Madrid. Her dress, from a leading Spanish fashion house, had been exquisite in its simplicity and style—and cleverly cut to disguise the growing presence of baby Isabella.

Zoe had hoped for an intimate reception, but with Mitch's fame that had not been possible. But it, too, had been perfect, with all his family and friends there. Mitch had flown over a number of her friends too, as their guests.

Louise, who was doing a brilliant job of steering The Right Note to further success as a full business partner, had been among them. She had moved into the Balmain apartment and taken over Einstein's care, as both she and Louise had agreed that he wouldn't have been happy with a move to another country. Louise had brought with her to the wedding a card signed with Einstein's pawprint that had made Zoe both laugh and cry.

When the time had come Amanda had insisted on flying to Madrid to be with Zoe and Mitch in the days after Isabella's birth, to help out. In an unobtrusive, loving way she had given her the help and support Zoe knew her own mother would have given her as she, in turn, had learned to be a mother.

Amanda had flown back to Australia once Zoe was managing motherhood on her own. Now she was back to watch Mitch's big game.

In marrying Mitch, Zoe had gained not only an adoring husband but also a warm, welcoming extended family that had filled the painful gap left by the loss of her own parents. It was an outcome she hadn't ever dreamed of.

Now she and Amanda looked again to the monitor, to see Mitch being interviewed on the pitch by a gaggle of sports media representatives. He switched effortlessly from English to Spanish in his replies, and Zoe was pleased with herself for being able to understand the Spanish. She had fitted right into life in Madrid and could happily converse with most people.

The main commentator for one of the big sports networks was interviewing Mitch now. Her husband's beloved face filled the screen.

'You've come back from your knee injury in spectacular form, Mitch,' the interviewer said. 'And I hear talk that you've been nominated as Footballer of the Year. Is this your greatest moment?'

Mitch looked directly into the camera. 'Yes, it's the greatest moment of my career,' he said, in that deep, familiar voice. 'But the greatest moment of my life was when my beautiful wife, Zoe, agreed to marry me, followed by the birth of our precious daughter, Isabella.'

Zoe stared at the screen long after Mitch had finished the interview. She knew he would be with her as soon as he could, and it wasn't long before she heard murmurs among the other guests in the VIP area that let her know he was on his way.

Dressed now in his team tracksuit, and wearing a medal on a ribbon around his neck, Mitch headed towards her, politely accepting the congratulations being showered on him but making it clear that he had eyes for only one person—his wife.

He swept her into his arms and hugged her close. Cameras flashed, but Zoe didn't care.

'We did it,' he said.

'*You* did it. I just cheered,' Zoe said. 'It was your victory.'

'It was *our* victory,' Mitch corrected her. 'I could never have done what I did this season without your love and support. Having you by my side has made all the difference. Thank you, wife.'

Mitch and his team had won the grand prize today. But Zoe knew the greatest prize of all was the love of her husband—and *she* had won it.

* * * * *